The Grievers

The Grievers

MARC SCHUSTER

THE PERMANENT PRESS
Sag Harbor, NY 11963

For information, address:
  The Permanent Press
  4170 Noyac Road
  Sag Harbor, NY 11963
  www.thepermanentpress.com

Library of Congress Cataloging-in-Publication Data

  Schuster, Marc—
    The grievers / Marc Schuster.
        p. cm.
      ISBN 978-1-57962-263-3
        1. Male friendship—Fiction. 2. Friends—Death—Fiction.
    3. Funeral rites and ceremonies—Fiction. 4. Bereavement—
    Fiction. 5. Interpersonal relations—Fiction I. Title.

  PS3619.C48327G75 2012
  813'.6—dc23   2012004249

Printed in the United States of America.

For Wei Han Chu
and Dan Barry

❧ CHAPTER ONE ❦

The telephone rang a second time, and Karen turned up her hands like a martyr revealing stigmata. The gesture was meant, I imagined, to imply that the pasty clumps of grayish glue and gooey shreds of wallpaper clinging to her rubber gloves rendered my wife incapable of dealing with the outside world—a silent argument that left me no choice but to counter her position with the irrefutable evidence of my own.

How am I supposed to answer the phone from all the way up here? I all but demanded, waving my trowel and heat gun at the stepladder beneath me. *Besides, this is serious business. Can't you see I'm using a power tool?*

A heat gun is hardly a power tool, Karen's raised eyebrows seemed to imply. *Climb down from your ladder and pick up the phone.*

Hardly a power tool? You plug it in, don't you? It makes a noise, doesn't it?

I conveyed these questions by scrunching my nose and curling my mouth into a sneer. Regardless of whether we were reading each other correctly, the conversation had, in the space of a heartbeat, gained enough momentum to erupt into a full-blown battle of frowns, shrugs, and eye-popping grimaces when the telephone rang a third time and reminded us why we were arguing in the first place.

Conceding defeat with an aggrieved sigh, Karen raced to the kitchen and answered the phone. When she returned a few seconds later with the gooey receiver pressed to her chest, I knew it was a call I didn't want to take.

"It's Mrs. Chin," she whispered.

I lowered my trowel and laid my heat gun on the top step of the ladder. The last time I'd seen Billy Chin was on New Year's Eve. We spoke for ten minutes before I noticed the line of stitches running from the heel of his hand to the dark recesses of his sleeve. Six months later, I received a note from his mother informing me that he had died. When I wrote back, I said she could call me anytime, night or day, if she wanted to talk. The offer looked great on paper, but as I climbed down from my ladder and reached for the phone, it dawned on me for the first time that the words might mean something.

"Charley Schwartz?" Mrs. Chin asked.

All I wanted was to hear that Billy's death had been an accident—that he was driving home from work one night when a tire came loose from the back of a truck and crashed through his windshield, or that he'd been held up at gunpoint or died pushing a child from the path of a speeding car, or, worst case scenario, that he'd uncovered a scandal at the health clinic where he'd been working and was permanently silenced by hired assassins. Part of me was even hoping that cancer was the culprit and that Billy had faced the disease with grace and elegance. I didn't need him to be a hero, exactly. A victim would have been fine, an unsuspecting pawn caught up in circumstances beyond his control. What I didn't want to hear from Billy's mother was what I already knew, so I clutched at my most elaborate fantasies even as she told me the particulars of her son's suicide.

He walked three blocks from home and jumped from the Henry Avenue Bridge, she said. A friend of the family identified the body. Like both of Billy's parents, the old man was a doctor, and his wife had taken care of Billy when he was a baby. When Billy's mother told me this last detail, her breath caught. He was always a happy boy—kind and generous, she said, like I'd written in the note I barely remembered writing. When the old man who identified the body asked why Billy jumped, those were the exact words his mother had used: because he was kind and generous, because he was thoughtful and polite, and he didn't want to burden his parents with the responsibility of coming home to an overdose.

Mrs. Chin spoke in a quiet, fragile voice.

I listened without saying a word.

There had been a girl in his life—a Japanese grad student who left Billy to take care of her mother in Osaka. Though Mrs. Chin said she could hardly blame the girl, the edge in her voice betrayed a hint of scorn. The same edge crept into her voice when she mentioned Billy's funeral. Of course I couldn't have gone, she said, because she wanted to keep the event small, keep it dignified and manageable, and therefore didn't invite anyone but family. Now that it was over, she wished I could have been there—that any of his friends from the Academy could have been there.

"He always loved the Academy," Mrs. Chin said.

I didn't know how to respond.

Founded in 1851, Saint Leonard's Academy was one of three schools in the greater Philadelphia area that could legitimately call itself the city's oldest prep school. Though no one at the Academy ever spoke the names of the other two institutions aloud, the official line was that one of them had relocated just beyond city limits after a fire in 1964 and that the other closed its doors for three months during the influenza pandemic of 1918. These accidents of geography and history allowed Saint Leonard's to use the phrase "under continuous operation in the city of Philadelphia" in ways that no other school could dream of. An informal poll of the young men who attended Saint Leonard's, however, revealed an altogether different, if not entirely subtle, distinction between their institution and the others. To wit, the other schools were full of pussies.

"It was a wonderful place," I said, omitting the fact that the unearned swagger of newly minted Academy grads had, over the years, led some to refer to the school as the Bastard Factory. "For all of us."

There was a long silence that I wanted to fill with anything but the sound of my own breathing, but all I could think about were the black stitches running up the inside of Billy's wrist and how I never said a word about them to anyone.

"You were a good friend," Mrs. Chin said eventually.

Though I suspected the opposite was true, I let it go. After we said goodbye, I hung up the phone and went back to work. Was I okay, Karen wanted to know as I climbed my ladder and reached for my heat gun?

I nodded and felt a lump growing in my throat.

"He jumped off a bridge," I said.

"Oh, Charley."

Karen stripped off her gloves, and my finger twitched on the trigger of the heat gun. The couch was shrouded in dirty sheets and plastic drop cloths, but Karen sat down anyway and motioned for me to join her.

I hated to stop working.

I wanted to plough forward.

I needed to put my house in order, but I couldn't get the image of Billy's stitches out of my head, couldn't stop thinking about his last desperate seconds, couldn't stop wondering if there was something I could have said or done, so I climbed down from my ladder, curled up next to my wife, and cried.

❦ CHAPTER TWO ❧

Saint Leonard de Noblac was a sixth-century monk whose prayers saw the queen of France through a difficult pregnancy. By way of compensation, King Clovis the Magnificent promised him all the land he could traverse via donkey within a nine-day period, and to sweeten the deal, the king also gave Saint Leonard the authority to free any prisoners he stumbled upon throughout the remainder of his life. At least, this is what I gathered from the slideshow I watched along with a hundred other awkward, pimply teenage boys on my first morning at the Academy.

"Make a goofy face when they do the class picture," the kid next to me said as a wizened Noblac friar extolled the virtues of Saint Leonard's faithful donkey, Maurice. "Trust me on this."

"Sure-footed and loyal," the friar said, barely audible over the clatter of slides as they cycled through the carousel. "Headstrong and determined, but never to the point of obstinacy."

The friar's name was Brother Timothy, and he cinched his brown robe at the waist with a coarse length of braided twine. Though he frequently referred to himself as a historian, Brother Timothy was only ever scheduled to moderate study halls and, when necessary, to sub for missing teachers. This was most likely due to the fact that his lectures invariably turned to the adventures of Saint Leonard and his donkey-cum-sidekick, Maurice. If the swim team defeated a major rival, Brother Timothy recalled a time when

Maurice and Saint Leonard crossed a raging river to deliver food to starving orphans. If the football team went down in defeat, Brother Timothy reminded us that Saint Leonard had been beset by wolves on more than one occasion, but had, by the grace of God, escaped with only minor cuts and bruises. And when a member of the custodial staff passed away in the spring of my sophomore year, Brother Timothy suddenly recalled that Saint Leonard was not only the patron saint of prisoners, blacksmiths, midwives, donkeys, thieves, travelers, good fortune, and the wheel, but of janitors and food-service personnel as well.

"Just as Christ rode a donkey into Jerusalem mere days before the crucifixion, so too did Saint Leonard pass through life on the most faithful of beasts," Brother Timothy droned that first morning as photographs of donkeys, many shot from conspicuously low angles, flashed across the screen behind him. "By the same token, so too do we expect you, the Raging Donkeys of Saint Leonard's Academy, to meet your destinies, both in the classroom and beyond, with fixed and firm dignity and aplomb."

"Raging Donkeys?" I said to the kid next to me.

"It's the name of our team," the kid said, clearly disgusted by my ignorance.

"Yeah, but why *Raging*?"

"Are you kidding? Have you seen the dicks on those things?" the kid said, raising his eyebrows in the direction of the stage where Brother Timothy stood silent behind a wooden podium, the thick lenses of his eyeglasses shining in the white glare of the slide projector. Behind him, more donkeys paraded across the silver screen, their undercarriages rendered more menacing with each shot by the photographer's growing fondness for the close-up. "Like the man said, fixed and firm."

The kid's name was Frank Dearborn, and except for his crooked nose, he looked like he'd be as comfortable shouting *Sieg Heil* at a Hitler Youth rally as he was pumping his fist and chanting the school's initials when the senior class president replaced Brother Timothy behind the podium and informed us that, as Raging Donkeys, we were nothing short of God's gift to the world.

"Check out that guy," Frank said, nudging me with his elbow as the houselights came up in the auditorium and the remaining chants of *S-L-A! S-L-A! S-L-A!* fizzled out like embers in a dying fire. "What's he doing here?"

I followed his gaze to one of the tallest people I'd ever seen in my life, a skinny black kid whose arms were a good six inches too long for his blue blazer. A white sticker over his heart read *Hi! My Name Is DWAYNE COLEMAN*. That no one else in the freshman class was wearing a name-tag meant that the kid must have recently worn the same jacket to some other event that did, in fact, require name-tags and had forgotten to take it off. That no one bothered to tell him about it meant that the joke was on him and would be for the foreseeable future. Tall and black were beside the point. To me, anyway, he'd always be the only guy in the room wearing a name-tag.

"What do you mean?" I said.

"I thought this school was segregated."

"Segregated?"

"Yeah. My dad said there were no blacks here."

"That's ridiculous," I said. "Where'd he get that idea?"

We were filing out of the auditorium now, and a doughy white kid whose heavy, labored breathing had been audible throughout Brother Timothy's presentation turned to me and explained what Frank was getting at.

"I believe he's referring to the fact that Saint Leonard's Academy is run by Noblac Friars," the doughy kid said. "In other words, your friend was expecting to see Noblacs today. Or, to make an obvious and perhaps unfortunate play on words, no blacks."

"Thanks," I said. "We're going to make funny faces when they take the class picture."

"I think I'll pass," the doughy kid said. "I don't want it biting me in the ass somewhere down the line."

"So, what?" Frank said. "You're running for president or something? Make a funny face for Christ's sake."

"My political aspirations are none of your business," the doughy kid said, shuffling away from us when his row started to move. "But, yes, one day you will see me in the White House—perhaps not as president, but certainly as a high-ranking aide-de-camp to whomever happens to be in office at the time."

"It's Packer, right?" Frank said.

"Correct," the doughy kid said.

"As in fudge?"

The doughy kid ignored the question, and though I didn't catch the reference, I laughed when Frank nudged me with his elbow.

"Get it?" Frank said. "Fudge Packer?"

"Yeah," I said. "Fudge Packer."

"What about you?" Frank said to a skinny Asian kid who was shuffling out of the row behind the doughy kid. "Are you a fudge packer, too, or are you going to make faces at the camera with us?"

The Asian kid glanced back at us but kept walking.

"Yeah, you," Frank said. "Rice Dick."

A few seconds too late, I figured out that Frank's fudge packer reference probably had something to do with anal sex. That combined with his calling the quiet Asian kid *Rice Dick* made me wonder whether I should distance myself from the guy before anyone assumed we were buddies.

"You're still going to do it—right, Schwartz?" Frank said, perhaps sensing a lack of resolve on my part as we filed into the gymnasium and Brother Timothy set up his camera on a tripod in front of the bleachers. "Make a weird face, I mean. You're cool with that, right?"

"Sure," I said.

"Awesome," Frank said. "I knew you were a good one."

Christ, I thought. It was like the guy was speaking a different language. Everything he said took forever to sink into my brain, and by the time I got it all decoded, I'd already agreed to hand over my lunch money, my good name, and anything else of value that I might have had in my possession, tangible or otherwise.

"A good what?" I asked, struggling to follow.

"A good Jew," Frank said.

"Oh," I said. "But I'm not Jewish."

"Hey, I'm not judging or anything," Frank said.

"I didn't think you were," I said, though he obviously was. "But, really, I'm not Jewish."

"Relax, Schwartz. It's nothing to be ashamed of."

"I'm not," I said. "I mean, I wouldn't be—if I were Jewish. Which I'm not."

"Then why are you getting so bent out of shape?"

"I'm not getting bent out of shape," I said, my voice rising a full octave.

"Whatever, Schwartz. Your secret's safe with me."

We climbed the bleachers, and Frank wandered off, his campaign to convince other kids to make faces at the camera kicking into full gear. Three weeks later, a poster-sized black and white photo of the freshman class was hanging in the foyer outside of our cafeteria. Jaws set, lips pursed, gazes fixed defiantly on some distant, manly horizon, my classmates did their best impersonation of serious adulthood while I stood in the front row with my eyes crossed and my cheeks puffed out like a blowfish.

"*Mazel tov*, Schwartz!" Frank called across the marble foyer as I stared at the photograph, cheeks burning, the only fool to fall into his trap. "Nice picture!"

"I believe I warned you about this," the doughy kid—whose name, I'd since learned, was Greg—said, breathing heavily as he made his way through the early morning crush of groggy boys and their overstuffed backpacks. "Now you'll never amount to anything."

"It could be worse," Billy Chin said, caught up in the crush. "Everyone *could* call you Rice Dick."

I hated Frank. I hated Greg. I even hated Billy at that point, despite the fact that I barely knew him. This wasn't the first humiliation in my life, but it was my first at the Academy, and it was a big one. All through grade school, my thick glasses and propensity for big words made me the target of boys who were much bigger than I was and who thought that professional wrestling was real. As a result, I suffered three black eyes, a chipped tooth, a broken nose, a dislocated shoulder, a scrape running from the inside of my elbow down to my belly button, two near drownings (one in a swimming pool and one in a toilet), a mild concussion, and countless noogies, wedgies, Indian burns, and wet willies, all between fifth and eighth grade. But I was never bitter—or not entirely so—because at the end of it all I knew I'd be the only kid from my graduating class who was moving on to Saint Leonard's Academy. To my mind, this meant starting over in a place where nobody knew me. It meant that I was making a fresh start, that I was forging a new identity, that I could turn myself into someone other than the geeky kid who talked funny and cried when other kids held him down on the ground and pressed his face into the mud. But now? After the class picture? Forget about it. Dwayne Coleman's name-tag was barely a blip on the radar by comparison.

In my mind, I was already tearing across the hall, rolling up my sleeves and breathing expletives as terrified fourteen-year-olds dove out of my way and hid behind trash cans and trophy cases to avoid the impending Armageddon. In my mind, I was swooping in on Frank from behind, grabbing him by the shoulder and spinning him around to face certain doom. In my mind, I was six inches taller than him and built like a lumberjack, and Frank was begging for mercy as I clutched the front of his shirt and cocked a fist mere inches from his trembling, terrified face.

"*Horse Feathers*," someone said.

The voice came from behind, so I spun around, impotent fists balled at my side, to find a kid whose round cheeks glowed like the moon and whose shoulders were dusted with big flakes of yellow dandruff. When I scowled at him, he made the face I was making in the class picture—crossed eyes, puffy cheeks, and fish lips—only to reveal a mouthful of heavy-duty orthodontic hardware.

"You're doing Harpo Marx, right?"

"Yeah," I said, feigning ennui. "Isn't it obvious?"

"That's pretty cool," the kid said. "I thought I was the only Marx Brothers fan around here."

Whatever the hell he was talking about, he was the only person in the entire school who didn't think I was an idiot. So I shook his hand when he offered it and assumed I was supposed to laugh when the bell rang for homeroom and he took off down the hall, stooped over like a walking question mark, knocking ash from an imaginary cigar, and singing, maybe to me, maybe to himself, maybe to the world at large, "Hello, I must be going. I cannot stay. I came to say I must be going. I'm glad I came, but just the same, I must be going!"

The kid's name was Neil Pogue. Twelve years later, he'd be the best man at my wedding. Nearly a year to the day after that, I'd get a call from Billy Chin's mother informing me that her son had committed suicide. Outside of crying in Karen's arms, telling Neil was the only thing I could think to do.

ℒ CHAPTER THREE ℒ

Whenever her mother asked what I was doing with myself that summer, Karen's answer usually started with something vague about research for my dissertation, touched briefly on our house and how desperately it needed our attention, elided over my congenital laziness, and ended squarely on a lie that had me working part-time in a bank.

The problem with Karen's phrasing wasn't so much the "working" part or the "part-time" part or even, surprisingly, the "bank" part. The problem was with the preposition. To say that I was working *in* a bank was a gross overstatement that implied a necktie, a sweater vest, air conditioning, and a working knowledge of the most basic laws of mathematics. To say that I was working *at* a bank might be a step closer to the truth, but only a small step that left far too much to the imagination. I might, for example, be mistaken for someone with the requisite training to carry a gun and prevent the occasional robbery. For that matter, I might also be mistaken for someone competent enough to push a broom or run a vacuum cleaner after everyone of consequence had gone home for the day. Plausible though all of these possibilities might have been for any other husband Karen's mother could have imagined for her daughter, they were slightly above my pay grade. The real truth was that I worked *in the general vicinity of* a bank. Or, more accurately, on the bank's front lawn.

The bank itself was the weakest link in a regional chain that still bore the name of the town where the first branch opened in 1889. What this meant in practical terms was that their rates were never especially good and that their ATM fees were based on the premise that the average customer had a balance of more than twelve dollars at any given moment. The way I fit into all of this was that the chain wanted to bring in more customers without spending a whole lot of money, so they invested in a dozen or so giant dollar sign costumes and left the individual bank managers to fill them—the only qualifications being a complete lack of ambition and an ass-load of time to kill. Fortunately for me, I had both, plus a Master's degree in English. My ace in the hole, however, was that the guy who hired me had graduated from Saint Leonard's Academy seventeen years before I did. This fact alone brought my resume to the top of the pile and meant that countless teens and high school dropouts would have to seek employment elsewhere that summer.

The idea, as far as I could gather, was for me to march back and forth in front of the bank dressed in the giant dollar sign costume so passing motorists would know that there was money in the building behind me. The costume was made of polystyrene and corrugated plastic and was studded with green sequins that glittered in the sun. It wasn't quite the size of a refrigerator box, but walking around in the thing was so awkward that it might as well have been. A little grate positioned just below eye-level let in light and air, and offered just enough peripheral vision to keep me from wandering off the lawn and into the path of oncoming traffic. Vents above my head and shoulders kept me from roasting alive as I marched along, hands poking out of the costume in white cotton gloves, one clutching a fistful of balloons, the other twitching in a half-hearted wave while my skinny legs wobbled back and forth and side to side in an effort to keep the whole bulky mess from toppling over.

Adding insult to injury, I also had to wear green stockings and rubber boots along with everything else because, in the opinion of my immediate supervisor, it didn't make sense for a dollar sign to be standing on the side of the road in bright white sneakers, particularly in June. Aesthetic concerns aside, the boots turned out to be a good idea because the lawn was always muddy, and it wasn't uncommon for the sprinklers to come on while I was on the clock.

My first day on the job, a tractor-trailer rumbled by, and the backdraft knocked me off my feet. I fell backwards onto the lawn and let go of my balloons and lay there for twenty minutes before anyone noticed my predicament. When a pair of tellers eventually came out of the bank to help me, they sighed audibly as their shoes squished across the muddy lawn.

"Lean into the wake of the larger vehicles," one of them said with an air of experience as they helped me onto my feet, "but know when to let up."

"And tie the balloons to your wrist," the other said. "Otherwise you'll keep losing them."

I tried to thank them for the advice, but they were behind me somewhere, and by the time I turned around, they were gone. Then the sprinklers came on, and I wondered what would happen if I tried to hitch a ride with the next tractor-trailer that came rumbling down the highway. The question, however, was rendered moot when I took two steps and slipped in the mud again. This chain of events established the pattern that carried me through the next few days, the only difference being that the tellers ignored me for exponentially longer stretches each time I fell over.

On the morning after my conversation with Mrs. Chin, I managed to pace the lawn and wave at oncoming traffic for a good fifteen minutes before the sprinklers started spitting at me and I slipped once again on the slick, muddy lawn. By that time, the tellers had apparently agreed amongst themselves to pretend that I didn't exist, so my only recourse was to set my balloons free, curl into a ball inside my big, boxy costume, and call Neil Pogue.

"Hey," I said into my cell phone when a chipper robot instructed me to leave a message after explaining that my best (and possibly only) friend was either unavailable or out of range. "It's Charley. I'm trapped in a giant dollar sign. Call me."

In the damp, sweaty dark of my costume, I tried not to think about the black line of sutures running up and down Billy Chin's wrist the last time I saw him. Instead, I tried to think of better times, but even the best were tinged with an aftertaste of teen angst and juvenile insecurity.

We never talked much when we were freshmen, but in our sophomore year, Billy and I shared a dead cat named Fascia. We kept her in a plastic bag on the back shelf of the biology lab and laid her body out on a yellow rubber mat every Thursday to see what secrets her hardened innards might reveal. The lab smelled of bitter formaldehyde and the acrid stench of overripe teenage boys fresh from the basketball court. Under the stark industrial glare of the halogen light rods glowing above us, the musculature beneath Fascia's skin took on a gray tint, and her eyes, sealed by rigor mortis, appeared to be squinting. Before we'd skinned her, Fascia was an orange tabby. Now she was a rubbery mass of bones and giblets in fuzzy white boots, an object lesson in how not to handle a scalpel.

"Billy Chin is Schwartz's lover," Frank Dearborn sang in a girly falsetto to the tune of Michael Jackson's "Billy Jean" while his lab partner, Andrew Taylor, executed a herky-jerky moonwalk, swiveled his hips, and grabbed his crotch. "He's just a boy who says that Schwartz is the one. But the cat is not their son."

If Frank had a single talent, it was playing Mad Libs with the pop charts. Per the unwritten rules of engagement at boys' schools everywhere, however, he could only employ this talent for purposes of torment, and he frequently awarded himself bonus points for raising doubts about the sexual orientation of his victims or for painting them in the most xenophobic of palettes.

"Hey, Chin!" Frank called from the lab table behind us. "I see your Schwartz is as big as mine."

His lab partner snorted, and I spun on my stool to give them both the stink eye.

"I don't get it," Billy said, studying our stained lab manual before making an incision in our cat.

"It's a line from *Spaceballs*," I said. "He's implying that I'm your penis."

"*Oy, gevalt*, Schwartz! Don't be disgusting. I'm saying that my dick is as big as you are."

"Whatever, Frank," I said and made a jerk-off gesture with my fist.

"Is there something you wanted to share with the class, Mr. Schwartz?" our teacher asked while my fist was still flying, mid-jerk, over my shoulder. His name was Phil Ennis, but we all called him Mr. Anus when he wasn't within earshot.

"No, Mr. Ennis," I said. "I don't have anything to share."

"Then perhaps you could walk us through today's dissection."

"Absolutely," I said, glancing at the lab manual in front of Billy. "I was just about to make an incision in our cat's—"

There were two cats on the page in front of me, each with a thick, black arrow pointing at the thing I was supposed to be cutting into. If I had looked closely, I probably would have noticed that one of the cats was a boy and that the other was a girl. But I didn't look closely. In fact, I barely looked at all, proceeding instead under the assumption that each diagram was more or less the same and that the labels were interchangeable.

"Your cat's what, Mr. Schwartz?" Ennis prompted.

"Our cat's scrotal sack," I said.

"That's very interesting," Ennis said, shuffling to our station in his powder-blue lab coat. "Let's all have a look, shall we?"

Billy nudged me with his elbow and tried, subtly, to point out that Fascia was a female, but it was too late. Even if the laws of biology rendered my search absurd, the growing throng of snickering boys gathered around my lab station forced me to at least take a stab at finding Fascia's scrotal sack. Fortunately for me, Billy had already done most of the dirty work of cutting away enough of the cat's innards to reveal a smooth, pinkish organ that bore a reasonable resemblance to a sack.

"Here we have the scrotal sack," I said, my hands sheathed in white latex gloves, my eyes scanning the instructions for mutilating this particular piece of the cat as laid out in the lab manual. "So our next step is to make an incision to reveal the specimen's testicles."

"Just so we're on the same page, Mr. Schwartz, are you saying that you found the specimen's scrotal sack *inside* its pelvic cavity?"

"I think so," I said.

"You don't sound so sure of yourself, Mr. Schwartz."

"Of course I'm sure of myself," I said, this time with feeling. "I found Fascia's scrotal sack inside her pelvic cavity."

Everyone laughed except for Billy.

"Then by all means, Mr. Schwartz, please continue."

Something small and lumpy shifted when I squeezed the organ. For a brief second, I imagined that a miracle had occurred and that, despite the odds, our cat had grown a pair of testicles in what was more than likely her uterus. But then I made a jagged incision, and a tiny, pinched face erupted from the glistening surface of the organ in question, appearing, despite being stillborn, to squint up at the sterile white lights of the biology lab.

"Look at that," Frank said. "Schwartz and Chin are parents."

Once again, everyone but Billy laughed until Ennis raised a hand for silence.

"This certainly is an interesting turn of events, Mr. Schwartz," he said. "Wouldn't you agree?"

"Yes, Mr. Ennis. I would."

"Stop me at any point if I'm mistaken, Mr. Schwartz, but you purport to have been making an incision in your specimen's scrotal sack, the function of which is to house and protect the testicles."

"Yes, Mr. Ennis."

"Yet when you made an incision in your specimen's scrotal sack, we discovered not testicles but kittens. Don't you find this the least bit curious, Mr. Schwartz?"

"I do, Mr. Ennis."

"You don't have kittens hiding in *your* scrotal sack, do you, Mr. Schwartz?"

"No, Mr. Ennis. I don't."

"And, to the best of your knowledge, Mr. Schwartz, your testicles don't, by any chance, bear a likeness to kittens, do they?"

"No, Mr. Ennis. My testicles don't look like kittens."

"Then how, Mr. Schwartz, do you explain the mysterious appearance of kittens in your specimen's scrotal sack?"

"Magic?" I said.

Ennis lowered his hand and turned his attention to Billy.

"Do you have anything to say about this strange turn of events, Mr. Chin?"

"It's a uterus," Billy said, looking at his shoes. "The specimen was female."

"Very interesting, Mr. Chin. Does your lab partner know the difference between males and females?"

"I don't know," Billy croaked.

"Indeed," Ennis said as the snickers hissing through the lab exploded into laughter. "One certainly wonders."

Ennis turned away, and a sea of pimply faces parted before him.

"Sorry," Billy whispered.

"Forget about it," I said.

"I didn't know what to say."

"Just forget about it, okay?"

I put down the scalpel, and Billy picked it up to finish the work I'd begun. He freed one dead kitten and then another from Fascia's hardened uterus. He laid them both on the yellow rubber mat next to their mother. A third was about to follow when Frank Dearborn cleared his throat and hummed the opening bars of "Billie Jean."

❦

THROUGH NO fault of my own, my cell phone played the theme from *The Jeffersons* every time I received an incoming call, so when Neil got back to me, the sweaty silence of my big, boxy costume was broken by the sound of a gospel choir singing about moving on up to the East Side, to a deluxe apartment in the sky.

"I won't even ask," Neil said when I answered.

"No, I wouldn't recommend it."

"Trapped in a dollar sign?"

"You said you wouldn't ask."

"Some of us have to work for a living, you know."

"You say that as if I took this job for shits and giggles."

"Knowing you? I thought you were lined up to teach summer school."

"Too much grading," I said. "I have a dissertation to write."

"And how's that coming along?"

"This isn't about my dissertation," I said. "This is about your best friend being trapped in the tomblike darkness of a giant polystyrene dollar sign. Are you going to help me or not?"

"I'm at work," Neil said.

"You work for the government," I told him. "Which means you work for the people, which means you work for me."

"You're being a dick. Are you aware of that?"

Neil had a point, but I had to keep pushing. The idea was to get him to meet me for lunch so I could tell him about Billy. My original plan had been to tell him over the phone, but every time I tried to call, I lost my nerve. Even now, the talking, witty, charming part of my brain was painting over Billy's suicide with layers and layers of thick, meaningless chatter. As if by not mentioning it, I could hold his death at bay. As if by refusing to say the words, I could keep Billy alive forever. Yes, Neil knew that Billy was gone, but he didn't know how our friend had died. That much information was my own private burden, at least as far as the two of us were concerned. Saying the words, relating the details and making them real, would force us into new territory. Given the chance, Neil and I could talk for hours and never say anything, but Billy's suicide took that option off the table.

"I'm asking for your help," I said. "If that makes me a dick, then I guess I'm a dick."

"I'm not saying you're a dick," Neil said. "I'm saying you're *being* a dick. There's a difference."

"So you'll help me?"

There was a long pause, and as the wheels of Irish-Catholic guilt turned in Neil's head, I told him where I was working and the easiest way to get there.

"That's a half-hour away," he protested, though we both knew how the conversation would end.

"Twenty minutes if you make the lights," I said.

"Can't you call Dwayne?"

"He's on duty," I said. "Either that or asleep. Besides, his solution would be to blast me out of this thing with his service revolver."

"What about Sullivan? Or Anthony Gambacorta? Why can't you bother one of them for a change?"

"Bother?" I said. "*Bother?* Sorry if I'm *bothering* you, Neil, but you're supposed to be my best friend."

"You know what I meant."

"If you can't help me, I'll understand, but my blood is on your hands."

"There's no emergency exit? No escape hatch?"

"It's a dollar sign," I said. "Not a school bus."

"Can't you shimmy out the bottom or something?"

"I think I'm suffocating, Neil. Growing lightheaded. How does it feel to be the last person ever to hear from me?"

"Christ," Neil said. "Give me an hour."

"If I don't make it, tell Karen I love her."

"Do me a favor," Neil said. "The next time I see you, remind me never to talk to you."

NEIL AND I never said much to each other in the months following our first encounter at the Academy. He was a face I'd see in the hallway, another kid in a rumpled blazer rushing from World Religions to Algebra. If we made eye contact, he'd drop lines from what I could only guess were Marx Brothers movies: *My boy, I think you've got something there, and I'll wait outside until you clean it up. Don't look now, but there's one man too many in this room, and I think it's you. The next time I see you, remind me never to talk to you.*

The best I could do whenever he'd say something like this was smile and hope it passed for being in on the joke. Not that anyone else was in on the joke, of course, but as long as *someone* at the Academy was under the impression, mistaken or otherwise, that I was in on *something*, I wasn't alone.

The first real conversation I had with Neil didn't happen until January of our freshman year. The North Philadelphia neighborhood where the Academy made its home had yet to succumb to the pull of gentrification, and when I stepped out into the blustery winter air after eight hours of being cooped up with hundreds of other pimply boys in our sweaty, smelly brick-and-mortar hotbox, the sun had already begun to sink low and red behind the crumbling row homes and dilapidated storefronts a block west of the school. At the far corner of the long, broken street, my usual bus sighed to a stop and opened its doors to three of my classmates. If I missed it, I'd have to wait another half hour in the growing darkness on a corner with no bench and only the cold, gray walls of the Academy to lean on, so I sprinted up the sidewalk in my battered brown oxfords and slapped at the door of the bus until the driver let me in.

"Say, I used to know someone who looked exactly like you," Neil said when I dropped, nearly breathless, into the seat next to him and the bus started to roll. "Emanuel Ravelli. Are you his brother?"

I smiled and hoped it would suffice, but the look on the kid's face said that he expected me to answer the question.

"The Marx Brothers, right?" I said.

"Yeah," Neil said. "Which one?"

"Which brother?" I said.

"No, which movie?"

"*Horse Feathers?*"

It was the only one I knew, and only because Neil mentioned it the first time he'd ever spoken to me.

"Close," Neil said. "*Animal Crackers.*"

"Right," I said.

"*For playing, we get ten dollars an hour,*" he said in a broken accent. "*For not playing, we get twelve. For rehearsing, we get a special rate. Fifteen dollars an hour. And for not rehearsing? You couldn't afford it.* You've seen it, right?"

"Once," I lied. "But it was a while ago."

The neighborhood rolled by—shattered stoops, sagging porches, windows of burnt-out houses covered over with plywood sheeting. Dripping red letters on the side of a rusty panel truck read *Angie's Soul Chicken*, and a life-size drawing of what appeared to be a rabid penguin stood guard at the door of a faded yellow bodega on the corner of Nineteenth and Porter. When a man with tiger stripes tattooed to his scalp crashed through the glass door of a pool hall on the next corner, the bus slowed to a stop just in time to get caught in the crush of locals that came pouring onto the street after him.

On the sidewalk, the man with the tiger stripes curled into a ball while a pair of muscle-bound goons, breathing steam in the cold winter air, beat him with the heavy back ends of their pool cues. In the space of a few heartbeats, the clientele of a neighboring bar swirled out onto the street wielding bats and broomsticks and anything else they could get a hold of, and it wasn't long before everyone's efforts at horning in on the proceedings erupted into full-blown mayhem.

As the bus shook and swayed with the swell of angry bodies, Neil shot me a glance, and I shrugged. Though a police officer had lectured the freshman class on keeping our wallets out of sight and avoiding dark alleys, he failed to mention what to do in the unlikely event that a riot should break out during the evening commute.

"I'm guessing it's like rock-paper-scissors," Neil said as a woman in a dirty apron cut a path through the fray with a soup ladle. "What do you think? Ladle scoops broomstick?"

"Right," I said. "Ladle scoops broomstick, and broomstick sweeps pool cue."

"Nice," Neil said. "But what does the pool cue do?"

"You don't want to know," I said, adopting the broken accent he'd used earlier.

Emerging from the knot of bodies, a man with a gash in his forehead pounded a fist against the front door of the bus. Without so much as turning his head, the driver opened the door while the passengers held their collective breath. When the man climbed aboard, he asked the driver if the bus went as far as the nearest hospital, and the driver said it stopped a block east of Saint Joseph's.

The man with the gash paused for a moment, then reached into his pocket for bus-fare. As he made his way toward the back of the bus, I glanced at the empty seat across the aisle from me, then glanced at the man, whose gaze met mine long enough for both of us to guess what would happen next.

The man took the seat.

I pursed my lips and nodded.

The man nodded back.

Red and blue police lights swept the darkening street. As the crowd dispersed and the bus started moving again, Neil pulled a white handkerchief from the inside pocket of his gray overcoat and passed it wordlessly to the bleeding man.

"I'M STILL not entirely clear on why you took this job," Neil said, squishing across the bank's muddy lawn to help me get back on my feet.

"Why does anyone take a job?" I asked, lying on my back. "I needed the money."

"But that's not the question," Neil said. "The question is why did you take *this* job?"

When he wasn't busy rescuing his friends from the consequences of their own foolish endeavors, Neil handled contracts for the Quartermaster Corps in their office just outside of Philadelphia. His wife Madeline, meanwhile, was finishing her doctorate in developmental psychology somewhere in Maryland. For the sake of fairness, at least in terms of the commute, they split the difference by living in Delaware, so I understood why the charm of my current job might have been lost on him.

"Flexibility?" I said.

"Try again."

"Potential for advancement?"

Not sure where Neil was standing, I reached out and groped blindly at the air in front of me, imagining that I looked like a turtle or an overturned insect from above.

"Sorry," he said. "Not until I get an honest answer."

"I told you before," I said. "I need time to work on my dissertation."

"Right," Neil said. "The dissertation."

"Ask your wife. It's a very complicated process."

"I know it is," Neil said. "I still don't believe you."

"Okay," I said. "I thought the job would be fun. Are you happy now?"

"Not yet," Neil said, but he took my hand anyway.

"What do you want to hear?"

"Fun's only half of it." He pulled on my arm, and I rose from the ground at an awkward angle. "And I'm not sure how much I buy that one either."

"Would you believe *funny*, then?"

"You took the job because you thought it would be funny?"

"Probably," I said. "Maybe. I guess."

"Hell of a reason to take a job."

"Look who you're talking to."

Finally standing on my own two feet, I pulled my arms back inside the dollar sign and lifted the boxy costume up and over my head. It was a variation on Neil's earlier suggestion of shimmying out the bottom, but if he took notice of this fact, he didn't let on.

"I still think there's more," Neil said. "Something you're trying to avoid."

"Please," I said. "You've been spending too much time with Madeline."

"I wish," Neil said.

"Too much time with her books, then. Do you feel like getting lunch?"

"I need to get back to work," Neil said, already turning away.

"No," I said. "I mean, wait. This is important."

Neil stopped and let out a sigh, then turned as if to ask what I wanted—or, more to the point, what I wanted *this time.*

"It's about Billy."

⚬⋊⋉⚬

Pills he could almost see, Neil said as we picked at tuna salad sandwiches and sipped iced tea in a booth at a chain restaurant in the strip mall across the street from the bank where I worked. Going to sleep and never waking up was one thing, but jumping from a bridge?

"Telling your legs to do this thing," he said. "That last second. I can only imagine."

"I don't want to think about it," I said.

"I went up in a helicopter once. You look down, and your bones freeze. You can't move a muscle."

My glittery dollar sign lay next to our table like an abandoned prop from *The Price Is Right.* Whenever I moved it or shoved it into the backseat of my car or slipped in the mud, a few sequins would flake off, but so far, the costume wasn't looking too bad—for a giant, glittery dollar sign, anyway. The only problem was that the costume made me look like a joke wherever I went, and I wasn't in much of a mood for joking.

"Do you remember New Year's Eve?" I said.

"Which part?" Neil said. "Packer hitting on Karen or you grabbing Madeline's ass?"

"That was an accident," I said.

"You don't grab someone's ass by accident," Neil said. "Especially when your wife is standing right next to her."

"That doesn't even make sense," I said. "What would possess me to grab your wife's ass when Karen was standing right there? If I really wanted to grab Madeline's ass, wouldn't I have waited until we were alone?"

"I don't know," Neil said. "You do a lot of things that don't make a whole lot of sense lately."

"This isn't about me," I said. "It's about Billy. Did you see his wrist or not?"

"No," Neil said. "I didn't."

"Well I did, and I didn't say anything."

Neil chewed on the inside of his lip, and our waitress breezed by the table to ask if everything was okay. Almost in unison, Neil and I turned to the woman and said that everything was great. Delicious, Neil added, though he'd barely touched his sandwich. In my mind, I thanked her for not asking any questions about my giant dollar sign, and in real life I asked for another glass of iced tea.

"He was hardly there," I said, looking away from Neil. "On the night of the party, he left after twenty minutes."

"He was in a bad place," Neil said.

"His fingers were so skinny," I said. "I remember thinking that. I remember looking at his hands and thinking that his fingers were so skinny, so bony, and then seeing the stitches in his wrist and not saying anything."

"You couldn't have known," Neil said.

I raised my eyebrows. "Stitches in his wrist? What else could it have meant? He spent the whole time telling me that he was going back to school for computers. Twenty minutes of this, and then he stopped and apologized and asked if he could use the phone, and all I could think about was how glad I was that he finally stopped talking."

"Who did he call?" Neil asked.

"His mother," I said. "She dropped him off at the party and came home to a ringing phone."

"She told you this?"

"She told me a lot of things."

"Like what?"

I shook my head. "He got off the phone and said he had plans. I knew it was a lie, but I let it go. It was the last time I ever talked to him."

Neil told me again that I couldn't have known, that our friend was in a bad place, that there was nothing I could have done, but all I could think about was Billy standing in the cold and waiting for his mother to come and pick him up while the rest of us laughed and drank and listened to loud music—while Greg Packer hit on Karen and I grabbed Madeline's ass.

WEARING THE dollar sign was easier than carrying it, so I climbed back inside the costume after Neil and I finished our sandwiches, and he held me steady as we crossed six lanes of traffic on our way back to the bank. If I did grab his wife's ass, I said as drivers leaned on their horns by way of telling us to get out of the intersection, I didn't mean it in a sexual way. I just thought it would get a few laughs.

"That's kind of sick," Neil said. "Is that your reason for doing everything?"

"Pretty much," I said.

"I feel sorry for Karen."

"You and me both," I said. "But that's why I need your help with this Billy Chin situation. I want to do something for him—something in his memory, anyway, but I don't want it to turn into a joke like everything else I do."

Neil warned me to watch out for the curb, and soon we were squishing back across the lawn in front of the

bank. Maybe we could raise some money and make a donation in his name, Neil said. He didn't mention the Academy,
but we both knew what he had in mind. He could make
a few calls and get our friends together for dinner some
night. We could say a few words about Billy and pass the
proverbial hat.

"Who are you thinking?" I asked.

"The usual crew, I guess. Dwayne Coleman and Sean
Sullivan. Anthony Gambacorta, if we can get a hold of him.
Greg Packer, of course."

"Of course," I said. "It wouldn't be a party without him."

Back at the Academy, the rumors about Greg and his
family sounded more like the stuff of soap operas and comic
books than the lives of any teenagers I'd ever met. In some
versions of the story, Greg's father was the heir to a massive
fortune, the child of a Rockefeller, a Carnegie, or a DuPont,
but he had to keep his relationship with Greg's mother a
secret for fear of losing any and all rights to his legacy. In
other versions, Greg had accidentally killed his father by
putting the family RV in reverse and backing over him on
the eve of a planned cross-country vacation to celebrate
Greg's fifth birthday. Depending on who passed the rumor
along, Greg's father could have been an artist, an inventor,
a hit man, a priest, a rock star, an oil man, an embezzler,
or a politician, while his mother's roles tended to alternate
between failed Olympic hopeful and disgraced nun.

When my turn came to build on the elaborately incon-
sistent mythology of Greg's life, I made him an heir to the
Holy Roman Empire and said that his father had devel-
oped a formula for tires that never wore thin, which led a
sinister cabal of tire manufacturers to have him eliminated
before he went public with his invention. That Greg never
confirmed nor denied the veracity of any of these rumors
only contributed to their weight as they echoed up and
down the polished halls of the Academy. What they all had
in common was that Greg's father was out of the picture

and that Greg and his mother enjoyed a steady unearned income, the limits of which were anybody's guess.

The real trouble with Greg started after we all graduated from the Academy and he fell into the habit of sliding from one disappointment to the next. His official story when he dropped out of Princeton was that he was homesick, but that didn't explain why it took him five years to complete a four-year degree at Saint Leonard's University in lieu of the ivy league education he'd always aspired to. Good scores on the LSAT got him into law school a year behind Neil, but by then he was so far out of the game that it didn't matter. Three car accidents, two of which involved collisions with parked cars, led to long periods of what Greg liked to call meditation and reflection but which largely consisted of chasing painkillers with bottle after bottle of Bud Light. When he wasn't busy hitting on my wife, he was, in his words, gathering strength for his next big move.

"What's he been up to lately?" I asked, almost afraid to hear the answer but knowing in a guilty way that it would make me feel better about my own life. "Aside from pining away for Karen."

"Nothing good," Neil said. "Failed the bar exam again, defaulted on his student loans, still fighting with his mother over whatever the hell they fight about."

"Is he at least good for a donation?"

"Sure," Neil said. "As long as I write the check. Sullivan's pushing for an intervention, by the way, and Dwayne wants to lure him into the city for a forcible commitment."

"He can do that?" I asked.

"In Philly? Please. The guy's a cop. It's the paperwork he's dreading."

We stood by Neil's car for a minute, not saying anything. When I caught my reflection in his windshield, I looked away. Dressed as a giant dollar sign, I looked like an idiot.

"So why do you think he did it?" Neil asked, keys in his hand. "Billy, I mean. Why?"

"I don't know," I said. "But I don't think he was like us."

"No," Neil said. "I guess not."

"He wasn't an asshole is what I mean. Not that we're assholes, exactly, but think about guys like Frank Dearborn. People like us, we knew how to deal with him—or we figured it out, anyway. People like Billy, though? He took things too personally. The Academy was sink or swim, and Billy could barely keep his head above water when guys like Frank were around. And that was just high school. Imagine being Billy in the real world. Imagine dealing with assholes every day and taking everything they did personally. Imagine how lonely he must have felt. How disconnected."

"He was in a bad place," Neil said.

"Yeah," I said. "He was in a bad place."

Neil opened his door and slid behind the wheel of his car. I gave him a wave as he pulled out of the parking lot, but his eyes were on the road ahead of him. As the sound of his engine faded into the hum of traffic on Route 202, I tramped out to my post and finished my shift on the muddy wet grass that stretched between the bank and the highway.

❧ CHAPTER FOUR ❧

I n the years following my graduation from the Academy, Phil Ennis gave up on watching his students mutilate dead cats in the name of science and migrated instead to the world of administration—first serving as Chair of Admissions, then as Vice President for Student Life, and finally as Director of Alumni Relations and Giving. It was in this final capacity that the man flourished. Unfettered from the constraints of dealing with pimply teens on a daily basis, he could spend the majority of his time composing long-winded pleas for cash, stock, real estate, and other gifts without ever having to worry about some misguided youth finding a cache of dead kittens in what he thought was a scrotal sack. What Ennis did have to worry about, however, was fielding calls from alums who expected him to remember their names despite the passage of time and the fact that they had yet to make a sizable donation to the school. Or, in my case, any donation whatsoever.

"Schwartz," Ennis said when I called from inside my dollar sign the day after my lunch with Neil. In the background, I could hear my former biology teacher tapping at a keyboard. After a brief pause, he pretended to retrieve my name from the soupy haze of his memory. "Class of 'ninety-one?"

"Yes," I said, playing along. "I'm flattered."

"We're a family, Schwartz. You know that. But as I recall, we haven't really heard from you lately."

"Sorry," I said. "I've been meaning to get in touch."

"A small consideration is all we ask. Pecuniary or otherwise."

"I understand," I said. "That's sort of why I'm calling."

"Sort of?"

"Do you remember Billy Chin?" I asked.

"Chin," Ennis said as if trying to put the name to a face.

"He was my lab partner in your biology class."

"Of course," Ennis said. "How could I forget?"

"He—passed away—about a month ago."

"Jesus," Ennis said. "How?"

"He killed himself," I said. "It was a suicide."

I told him everything I knew, including how to get in touch with Mrs. Chin in the event that he wanted to forward his condolences, and Ennis said that he'd include a death notice in the next issue of *The Academic*. Slick, shiny, and full of pictures, the Academy's alumni journal arrived in the mail four times a year. Though Karen once figured out that Ennis's face appeared, on average, once every three pages, the majority of the magazine was dedicated to spreading the good news that Saint Leonard's was and always would be the region's strongest bastion of Noblac ideals—namely courage, loyalty, faith, and intellect.

"A few of us were thinking of making a donation in Billy's name," I said. "Maybe setting up a scholarship fund. Is there a protocol for that kind of thing?"

"Absolutely," Ennis said. "But it runs into money. To make it worthwhile, we're talking two million up front."

"Dollars?" I said.

"And that's just to get the ball rolling. Which isn't to say we can't explore other avenues. A few years back we did a survey and found that fewer than thirteen percent of our students come from within city limits. Given our reputation as Philadelphia's oldest prep school, that's completely unacceptable, so we set up a scholarship to get more Philly boys in the door. You can always earmark whatever you pool together for that one, assuming Billy lived in

Philadelphia. Or, if you prefer, you can assign your donation to an extracurricular activity like the drama society or the chess team. That's how you two met, right? On the chess team?"

"No," I said. "I was never on the chess team."

"At any rate, we have plenty of options."

Sensing, perhaps, that there was no real money to speak of on my end of the conversation, Ennis repeated his condolences before cutting me loose. In the cramped, muggy darkness of the dollar sign, I snapped my cell phone shut and checked the time. Relieved that my shift was almost over, I crawled out the bottom of my costume and dragged it to the parking lot where my boss, the Associate Manager, was taking a cigarette break.

"No balloons today?" she said as I shoved the dollar sign into the backseat of my car.

"I had some earlier, but I let go of them when I fell."

"Didn't Terry tell you to tie them to your wrist?"

"Is Terry the guy who smells like sausage?"

The woman nodded. Her name was Sue. She had a different blue suit for every day of the week and an apparent fetish for ruffled blouses. The effect, heightened by her brittle blonde hair and papery skin, was to make her look like she had a part-time gig playing in a gloomy version of the Partridge Family. When I looked at her, I couldn't help wondering if this was what the future held for me as well—the daily, soul-sucking grind of a real job, the prospect of each year blending into the next until they all congealed into a pointless, washed-out blur. Was this what killed Billy, I wondered, as Sue exhaled a plume of smoke? Did he see where his life was headed—where all of our lives were headed—and opt instead to bag the game altogether?

"The balloons are part of the image," Sue said. She worked directly under the Academy alum who gave me the job, and she more or less understood the two most fundamental aspects of my position—namely that it was pointless, and my connections meant that firing me would be more trouble than it was worth. Nonetheless, she wanted me to at least play along. If Sue had to pretend that I was legitimately employed, then I had to at least make the occasional gesture toward doing the same. "We want people to associate banking with fun."

"Who doesn't associate banking with fun?" I said.

"Just tie the balloons to your wrist, okay?"

I was tempted to ask where lying flat on my back on the side of the highway fit into Sue's hierarchy of things people should associate with banking, but it was the kind of wise-ass remark that would make my wife cringe when she eventually found out about it, so I kept my mouth shut. If nothing else, being married made me think twice before saying anything that might otherwise get me into trouble.

WHEN I got home, Karen had stripped the last of the wallpaper from our living room walls and was beginning to work her way up the stairs. The woman who lived in the house before us had been a heavy smoker, and her white wallpaper had, over the years, turned ugly shades of yellow and brown where the walls met the ceiling. So we burned lead paint away from the woodwork, scraped the wallpaper with a wire brush and razor blades, and soaked the walls with hot, soapy water until the pasty paper came away from the plaster in thin, sticky layers that reminded me of phyllo dough. In the can, the paint we had chosen looked like melted chocolate ice cream.

"They want two million dollars," I said, kneeling one step below my wife and scouring the wallpaper with a wire brush. "If we want to set up a fund in Billy's name, that's how much we'll need."

"I guess we'll be selling the vineyard, then."

Karen was wearing cutoff jeans and a lime-green tee shirt that her students had given her as a souvenir for chaperoning the senior prom. When she wasn't teaching, she was grading papers, and the only break she ever took from grading was to vent her frustration on our walls and woodwork. Considering the amount of wallpaper lying in shreds on our living room floor, my guess was that her students still couldn't quite articulate the difference between Realism and Romanticism.

"I'm serious," I said. "Two million."

"It's the thought that counts, Charley. Make a donation in Billy's name. Give what you can. It's not like the Academy won't take your money."

"Of course they'll take my money," I said. "That isn't the point. The point is respect. I want them to know that I can do this, that I'm not a total—you know."

"A total what?" Karen said.

"Fuck-up."

"Who said you were a total fuck-up?"

"No one," I said. "Besides, this isn't about me. It's about Billy."

"Okay," Karen said, tugging at a strip of wallpaper. "As long as it doesn't turn into another one of your crusades."

"Crusades?" I said. "What are you talking about?"

"Your fixation with apostrophes, for example."

"That's justified," I said. "And I'd hardly call it a crusade. I just happen to have a deep and abiding respect for the English language."

"We can't eat at Fernando's anymore," Karen said.

"Are you kidding? I did them a favor."

"You pissed off Fernando."

"The sign said *special's*—with an apostrophe S. Besides, there *is* no Fernando. That was the bartender."

"Whoever it was, you could have at least apologized when he told you to get away from his sign."

"Apologize for what? I saw a problem and I fixed it."

"I stand corrected," Karen said. "You're the Albert Schweitzer of punctuation."

"I'm not on a crusade," I said.

"Fine," Karen said. "You're not on a crusade."

For the next hour, we scraped, scoured, soaked, and scrubbed as the yellow wallpaper gradually gave way to gray, pockmarked plaster. At the bottom of the stairs, the radio was tuned to a classical music station. If either of us spoke, it was only to trade a scraper for a wire brush. Beyond that, we worked in silence.

❧ CHAPTER FIVE ❧

Neil made a reservation for twelve at a restaurant that was mutually inconvenient for everyone. After driving nearly an hour north along the gray corridors of the Pennsylvania Turnpike, I spied an electric sign boasting eighty-seven varieties of nachos and knew I was in the right place. That *nachos* was spelled with an apostrophe S didn't make me cringe so much as it forced me to hold my tongue as the hostess seated me alone at a long table beneath a red bicycle that dangled precariously from the ceiling on super-fine strands of fishing line.

For the next ten minutes, I sipped iced tea and made a show of studying the menu while conversations buzzed all around me. When the waitress paused at my table to ask if I needed a refill, my sense was that the question had less to do with my drink than the hungry patrons-in-waiting eyeing the vast expanse of real estate in front of me with a mix of envy and outrage.

"Hey, big boy," I said when Neil arrived. "How about a drink?"

"Sorry," Neil said. "I never take a drink unless somebody's buying."

"*Duck Soup?*" I asked.

"Close," Neil said. "*Animal Crackers.*"

Everything I knew about the Marx Brothers I'd pieced together from sound bites, documentaries, Trivial Pursuit, and conversations with Neil, but I'd never actually seen one of their movies in its entirety. Like anyone even vaguely familiar with their work, I knew Groucho's iconic mustache and glasses on sight, guessed that his cynical outlook on life had earned him his nickname, and understood that the animated stork in the Vlasic Pickle commercials was modeled after his trademark stoop, deadpan delivery, and incomparable cigar-play. I knew that Harpo didn't talk, that he wore a curly wig, and that he honked a horn whenever he got excited. I knew that Chico spoke in a broken accent and once told a reporter that he'd been Italian until he saw what they did to Mussolini and subsequently decided to become Greek. I knew that Zeppo had starred in only a handful of films, always playing the straight man, and that Gummo had quit the act before they made it to the silver screen.

I'd learned all of this through the kind of passive research that makes renaissance men of us all—a PBS special on a rainy Sunday here, a zero-context rant from my grandfather there. Fortunately or not, this was how I learned pretty much everything in my life. I never read the Beats, I only read about them. I never went to war, but I saw it on TV. I never played football, but I looked forward to every new version of *Madden NFL* to hit the shelves. And the closest I've come to a psychedelic experience is reading *The Doors of Perception*. Some people immerse themselves in the things they love, the things that excite them, the things that pique their curiosity. At best, I'm the kind of person who dips a toe in the water, but more often than not, I'll settle for hearsay, opting always to remain a safe distance from whatever it is that holds my attention.

"Nice place, by the way," I said, glancing at the bicycle above us.

"Sorry," Neil said, apologizing before I could really start to complain—about the drive, about the wait, about the superfluous apostrophe. "Anthony had a coupon."

"So he's coming?" I asked.

"Actually, no," Neil said. "He just called to bail on us. Something about a *Dukes of Hazzard* marathon."

Back at the Academy, Anthony Gambacorta was a pudgy kid with thick glasses who used to hang out in the light booth and share his extensive pornography collection with the stage crew while the Carrot and Stick Drama Society butchered the likes of Arthur Miller and Eugene O'Neill in the theater down below. During our sophomore year, he made a name for himself when he replaced all the posters advertising an upcoming production of Bock and Harnick's *Fiorello!* with counterfeits that read *Fellatio!* instead. The fact that nobody caught the mistake until a reporter for the *Philadelphia Inquirer* spotted it on the last night of the show didn't do much for the school's reputation; but an insatiable appetite for porn kept everyone in the know from ratting Anthony out even when the administration threatened to pull the plug on the drama program altogether.

Anthony was also responsible for programming my cell phone to play the theme from *The Jeffersons* whenever it rang—a gift, he said after he'd done the deed, for my previous birthday, which he'd missed by two months. It was the last time I'd seen him in the flesh, and the only reason I was disappointed that he couldn't make it to dinner with us was that I wanted him to change my ringtone back to whatever it was before. Not that I couldn't figure it out for myself. I was simply standing on principle. Anthony was the one who put the damn ringtone on my phone in the first place, so he'd also be the one to take it off, come hell or high water.

"The good news is that he's working on a musical," Neil said.

"And the bad news?"

"It's an adaptation of *Hogan's Heroes*. He's calling it *Down in the Stalag*."

"Is he at least good for a donation?"

Neil shrugged.

Before he could say anything, Greg Packer arrived on the heels of our waitress, whom he instructed to return with a pitcher of margaritas and a plate of nachos. We were here to honor a fallen comrade, he added, so she should limit her intrusions to a bare minimum and keep an eye out for the remainder of our party. We were in mourning, he stressed—stricken with grief—so if she could please hurry up with the margaritas and nachos, he'd make it worth her while.

"Gentlemen," Greg said, acknowledging our presence only after the waitress hurried away. "Given the circumstances, it is, of course, with a heavy heart that I dine with you this evening, but I am also pleased to report that my personal fortunes have taken a turn for the better. To wit, I think I'm in love."

"Again?" Neil said. "Who's the lucky lady?"

"And please don't say Karen," I added.

"Considering our larger purpose this evening, I'll ignore that remark and say only that her name is Evangeline and that she lives in Chicago."

"Illinois?" I said.

Greg looked at me as if I were something he'd stepped in. Yes, Illinois, he said in a tone that might have been justified if he'd ever come close to realizing the grandiose dreams of his childhood. As it stood, however, he was just another unshaven slob in a rumpled blue blazer who lived with his mother and spent his days trolling the Internet for potential mates who might, in his words, extend the Packer line by agreeing to carry his seed. If he had any regrets that it wasn't the future he'd imagined for himself back at the Academy, he never let on. Instead, he proceeded to behave as if the world had, in fact, made good on the unspoken promise it makes to all children—that we can be anything, that we can go anywhere, that we can do whatever we want as long as we want it badly enough.

When our waitress returned with a pitcher of margaritas, she asked how many glasses we wanted. It was, I imagined, her subtle way of inquiring as to whether or not we needed such a large table, but Greg shot her down with a casual wave of his hand as if to say he couldn't be bothered with petty details.

"Is it me, or does our girl seem a little infatuated?"

"I think it's you," Neil said as the waitress conferred with the hostess, the hostess conferred with the manager, and all three joined the hungry crowd at the front of the restaurant in eyeing our table with mounting suspicion. "And I'm also beginning to think that we need a smaller table."

"Nonsense," Greg said. "You reserved a table for twelve, so we'll dine at a table for twelve."

"That was probably a mistake," Neil said. "I thought we'd get a bigger crowd."

"So it's only us?" I said.

"Irrelevant," Greg said. "If the people out there had planned ahead, they'd already be seated. The fact of the matter is that they left too much to chance and now they're paying for it. If we give up our table now, we'll only be rewarding their indolence."

"Sean's coming," Neil said. "But only because I told him you were interested in buying a Volkswagen."

"Great. So now I have to suffer?"

"Don't talk to me about suffering," Greg said. "I know suffering."

"Getting into a few fender benders doesn't amount to a life of suffering," I said.

"Fender benders?" Greg said, already pouring himself a second drink. "Is that what you heard? Because that particular turn of phrase hardly does justice to the horrors I've been through. Just waking up in the morning is sheer agony. I need a pill to get out of bed. And taking a shower? Forget about it. In fact, it's a minor miracle that I'm even sitting here this evening."

"There's also a decent chance that Dwayne might come," Neil interjected. "But other than that, I think it's only us."

"Will he be in uniform?" Greg asked.

"I don't know," Neil said. "Why?"

"Because if he is, the wait staff might assume that the fallen comrade to which I alluded was also a police officer, and that, by extension, we're all, like Dwayne, members of the force. This perception, false though it may be, will foster the impression that we're deserving of at least a modicum of recognition and, thus, that a table for twelve is a small price to pay for the privilege of serving us. We will, in short, be regarded as heroes, and there's a better than average chance that we'll receive a free round of drinks before the night is through."

"That's idiotic," I said.

"On the contrary," Greg said. "It's human nature. Just watch."

Greg gestured in the direction of the hostess stand where Dwayne Coleman stood in full uniform, towering over the hostess, whose demeanor toward our table went in the blink of an eye from wary to enthusiastic as she pointed our friend in the right direction with a wide, welcoming smile. Watching him cross the crowded floor, I thought about the race joke Frank Dearborn made at his expense on our first day at the Academy: *I thought this school was segregated!* As was the case with most of my friends from that era, the only reason I knew Dwayne at all was that we were both friendly with Neil. Though we never talked much at the Academy, Dwayne and I had a standing date to drink beer and wallow in self-pity on his father's back porch every other Friday night in the jobless, womanless, directionless summer after college.

As if to prove Greg's theory, our waitress appeared with a plate of nachos as soon as Dwayne took a seat. Ignoring the eight empty chairs at our table, she asked Dwayne if she could get him anything to drink, and he ordered a glass of water. He was going on duty in a few hours, he said when the waitress left and Greg offered him a margarita, so alcohol was out of the question. When the waitress returned with Dwayne's water, she also brought Sean Sullivan, who handed me his business card by way of saying hello.

"I know this isn't the best time," Sean said. "But Neil tells me you're in the market for a new car."

"You're right," I said. "It's not the best time."

"I only mention it because I'm concerned. Are you still driving that old Saturn?"

"I wouldn't call it old, exactly." A leprechaun winked in the corner of the card. On weekdays, Sean put his graduate degree in counseling to work by helping the mentally and physically infirm find jobs in the private sector. On weekends he put dents in his student loans by selling cars to the same demographic. "I prefer to think of it as broken in."

"All the more reason to trade up," Sean said. His voice had the shrill tenor of a pennywhistle and the urgency of a police siren, and he'd recently taken to sporting a goatee to highlight the boundary between his neck and chin. "A few years from now, we'll laugh you right off the lot."

"I'll take my chances," I said, pocketing his card. "Right now I have bigger things to worry about."

"Indeed," Greg Packer said. "Our fallen comrade deserves our full and undivided attention."

"And let's stop with this *fallen comrade* shit," I said. "He was our friend, for Christ's sake. Would it kill you to use his name?"

"My apologies," Greg said. "I didn't realize you two were so close."

I opened my mouth but didn't say a word, ashamed to admit that Billy and I were never close at all. Friendly, yes, especially back at the Academy, but I'd be surprised if we spoke more than three times since graduation. Always polite, always cordial, but always with the ulterior motive— on my part, anyway—of escaping the conversation. In fact, the only reason I invited him to my New Year's Eve party was to put off meeting him for dinner the night before

Thanksgiving, and the only reason we'd planned to meet up the night before Thanksgiving was that I'd been putting off invitations to have lunch with him since the previous summer. In some ways, it was my main reason for having the party—not to see Billy so much as to gather all of my acquaintances together and not have to talk to any one of them for too long.

If nothing else, I'm a very social misanthrope.

"Remember how he used to bring a wok to school?" Sean asked.

"It wasn't a wok," I said. "It was a bucket."

"Some kind of Asian thing," Sean said. "Greens and rice every day. The kid should have outlived us all."

"It wasn't Asian," I said. "And he wasn't a kid. He was an adult like the rest of us."

"I'm saying *then*," Sean said. "He was a kid *back then*. Christ, Charley, do you have to be so goddamn difficult all the time?"

Greg signaled the waitress for another pitcher of margaritas. Neil asked if he thought it was such a good idea, but Greg brushed Neil's concerns aside with a flick of his wrist. He'd made arrangements for a ride, he said.

"A cab?" Neil asked.

"In a manner of speaking."

"He bit into a grub," I said, still caught up in our previous conversation. "He was eating lunch one day, and when he looked down there was half a grub on his plate."

"On his *plate*?" Dwayne asked. "You said it was a bucket."

"Fine," I said. "His bucket."

"So, what?" Sean asked. "Was this some kind of Asian thing? Like eating grasshoppers in Mexico?"

"No," I said. "It was an accident. That's my whole point."

"You'd think he'd be more careful," Dwayne said. "Using chopsticks and all."

"He didn't use chopsticks," I said. "He used a fork."

"I remember chopsticks," Greg said. "And Sean's right. It was a wok."

"The point I'm trying to make is that he ate a grub one day, and I watched him do it," I said. "I could have stopped him, but I didn't. I saw the grub, and I saw him going for it, but I let him eat it anyway."

"When you say *grub*?" Neil said.

"A worm, okay? I let Billy eat a worm."

"Like an earthworm?" Sean asked.

"Like a maggot," I said. "Only bigger."

"And you didn't try to stop him?"

"What was I supposed to say?"

"I don't know," Dwayne said. "How about, 'Hey, Billy, there's a giant goddamn maggot in your lunch.' "

"You're right," I said. "I should've stopped him."

THE WAITRESS brought our second pitcher of margaritas, and soon we were meandering across the same conversational terrain we'd been treading for the past decade: Anthony Gambacorta's extensive porn collection, Brother Timothy's fascination with donkey dicks, and the unfounded rumor that a certain modern language teacher left in the middle of a semester because she was pregnant with a certain friar's love child. When our perverted walk down memory lane started to repeat itself, Neil took a moment to remind us once again, and more gently than I'd managed, why we were gathered. We wanted to make a donation to the Academy in Billy's name, he said—because he always loved the school, because he always lived the Noblac ideals, because our friendship meant the world to him. I added that I'd spoken to Phil Ennis, and though a scholarship in Billy's name was out of the question, we could at least make a respectable donation to the fund the Academy was setting up for Philly boys.

"What if we bought the school a ping-pong table?" Sean suggested. "For the student lounge. I know some people. We can get it wholesale. Add a brass nameplate for twenty bucks or so? It could be a nice gesture."

"We're thinking more of a cash donation," Neil said.

"If I recall correctly—and there's no reason to believe I don't—Billy *did* play a lot of ping-pong," Greg said. "So Sean's idea certainly has merit."

"When did Billy play ping-pong?" I asked.

"Every day," Sean said. "At lunch. I remember like it was yesterday."

"You also remember that he brought a wok to school."

"Even so, I think it's an appropriate gift."

"Whatever you guys decide is fine with me," Dwayne said. "Put me down for twenty bucks."

"Twenty?" I said.

"Okay, thirty."

"You're joking, right?"

"We were hoping everyone could at least give a hundred," Neil said. "It's not a lot, but at least it's something."

"Not a lot?" Dwayne said. "I'll go as high as fifty, but that's it."

"This isn't an auction," I said. "We're talking about a friend of ours."

"I still think we should go with the ping-pong table," Sean said.

"We're not buying a ping-pong table," I said.

Neil shot me a glance that said I was losing my cool, but it was too late. My cool, if I ever had any, was long gone, and I felt as if I were watching myself turn rabid in a low-budget nature documentary. My eyes went wide. My pulse turned rapid. My hands started shaking. I could hear my voice getting louder as I spoke, but even the prospect of drawing unwanted attention to myself and my fellow Academy grads didn't slow me down.

"You understand that Billy's dead, right? He jumped off the Henry Avenue Bridge because people like us never gave him the time of day. And now that we're trying to do something nice for him, all you care about is trying to figure out the cheapest way to do it. He was our friend, for Christ's sake. And you want to buy a ping-pong table? No wonder they call it the Bastard Factory. You guys are a bunch of—cheap—fucking—bastards."

The last words escaped my lips in stuttering staccato bursts, and our waitress hurried to the table to see if everything was okay. Before I could turn to her and say that, no, everything was decidedly *not* okay, Neil apologized for my outburst and asked for the check.

"You're upset," Sean said. "I understand. Maybe we should continue this conversation another time. You do have my card, right?"

"Yes, Sean. I have your card."

"Then call me sometime, okay? You'd be amazed at how a new car can change your outlook on things."

Neil raised a discreet hand to keep me from leaping out of my seat, but it didn't matter. Something inside me had broken, and there was nothing I could do to fix it, so I slumped forward in my chair and told Sean I'd be in touch as he dropped a few bills on the table and said that he'd had a good time.

"As have I, gentlemen," Greg said. "But I fear I've kept Mother waiting long enough."

"Your mother still waits up for you?" Dwayne asked.

"God, no," Greg said. "She's waiting in the car."

Greg opened his wallet and laid a ten-dollar bill on the table. He'd only had a hamburger, he said by way of explanation. In fact, we probably owed him some change, but given the somber nature of the occasion, he was willing to let it slide.

"Two words," Dwayne whispered as Greg followed Sean out the door. "*Forcible commitment.* We can do it tonight. Just lure him inside city limits, and we'll lock him away."

"Maybe some other time," Neil said.

"Suit yourself, but you know where to find me if you change your mind."

Dwayne laid some money on the table. He'd love to stick around, he said, but his shift was starting in a little over an hour. Promising to send Neil a check, he rattled his keys and left the two of us alone at our long, empty table.

"That was a great success," Neil said, aping Groucho Marx as he totaled up the bill. "One more like that, and I'll have to sell my body to science."

"*Animal Crackers?*" I said, taking a shot in the dark.

"Close," Neil said. "*The Cocoanuts.*"

✤ CHAPTER SIX ✤

All told, we raised $470. Neil kicked in an additional thirty to make it an even five hundred, and I wrote a brief letter to accompany the check that we forwarded to the Academy. The letter said that we'd always remember Billy as the kindest of souls and that our gift was the least we could do to honor his memory. It also listed the names of everyone who had contributed to the sum, including Greg Packer, whose donation of fifty dollars came in the form of a promissory note to Neil, and Anthony Gambacorta, who sent a check signed by his mother and a pledge of points on the back end of any and all future productions of *Down in the Stalag*. Though I didn't know what this last piece of information meant, I included it in the letter anyway because it sounded like the kind of thing that Phil Ennis would love to mention on the AlumNotes page of *The Academic*. When he called for clarification three days after I mailed the check, however, all I could tell him was that I thought points had something to do with the amount of money a movie made after all was said and done.

"I know what points are, Schwartz," Ennis said. "I want to know how many we're getting."

"I'm not sure," I said, carefully pacing the lawn in front of the bank, one arm tucked inside my giant dollar sign so I could hold the phone to my ear, the other arm held limply aloft by the bouquet of brightly colored balloons tied to my wrist. "But I can probably find out."

"And you have this in writing? That Anthony pledges a certain number of points on the back end of this—what is it? A movie or something?"

"It's more of a musical," I said.

"Broadway?"

"Not exactly."

"So we're looking at what in terms of box office?"

"I have no idea," I said. "Did you get the check I sent?"

"We received *one* check," Ennis said. "From Neil."

"Actually, that was from both of us. All of us, in fact—everyone I mentioned in the letter. We thought it would be easier just to collect the money and write a single check."

"You mention four people in this letter," Ennis said. "In addition to yourself and Neil."

"Right," I said, quickly counting my friends on the fingers of one hand. "That's six altogether."

"Yet the check was for five hundred dollars."

I sensed an unspoken *only* in Ennis's statement and reminded him that he was also getting a percentage of any profits Anthony Gambacorta might make on *Down in the Stalag*. I was about to add that the promise of points on any musical based on *Hogan's Heroes*—even one that had yet to be staged—was like having money in the bank, but the backdraft of a passing tractor-trailer knocked me off my feet before I could say it.

"—a little disappointing," Ennis was in the middle of explaining when, lying flat on my back, I regained my bearings and pressed the phone to my ear. "But you'll be pleased to learn that we still have options."

"Options?" I said.

I pulled my free arm inside the dollar sign and switched my cell phone from one hand to the other. The only problem was that the balloons were still tied to my wrist, and whenever anything larger than a bicycle whizzed by, the balloons tried to follow, tugging at my arm and yanking the phone away from my ear until I wrestled it back. As a result, I only caught about half of what Ennis said next, and even then, I could barely make sense of it.

"We can still—situation—advantage," he explained. "Letter—finesse. Classmates. Details. The key is—working. Noblac ideals—friendship—donkey—interested parties. You— Pogue. Rank—horn—Friday?"

"Absolutely," I said, switching hands again.

"Then let's plan for noon," Ennis said.

"Right," I said. "Friday at noon."

"Pogue, too?"

"Probably," I said, though I didn't know what I was agreeing to. "But I'll have to run it by him first."

"Good," Ennis said. "Unless I hear otherwise, we'll see you then."

"We?" I said, but Ennis had already hung up.

THAT NIGHT, I paced our narrow hallway while Karen stripped more of the old, yellowing wallpaper from the walls. Given my brooding personality and general uselessness around the house, it was hard to say what she ever saw in me. To this day, the best answer I can give is that my life has been marked by short, random bursts of inspiration and activity, followed by extended periods of coasting, disenchantment, boredom, lethargy, and, eventually, surrender. Unfortunately for Karen, she happened to meet me while I was on the upswing. Two years out of college, I'd ditched three jobs and decided that the next mountain I wanted to climb would be graduate school. This time, I told myself, I'd give it my all. This time, I wouldn't cut any corners. This time, I wouldn't stop at simply buying the books—I'd actually read them and make notes and form study groups to make sure I got the most out of my education.

As it turned out, Karen was the only person who joined my study group, and by the time we started dating, I had her convinced that I knew what I was doing. I wasn't going to stop at the Master's Degree, I told her. I was going to go on for my Doctorate. From there, I'd probably do some post-doc work (whatever that was), get some academic writing under my belt (it sounded plausible at the time), settle into a tenure-track position at a small liberal arts college (why not?), and spend the rest of my life discussing the significance of the green light at the end of Daisy's dock in *The Great Gatsby*. But then came the Ph.D. program and all the books I had to read, and all the books about the books, and all the talk from all of the professors about how bad the job market was, and as my dreams started slipping further and further away, I stopped trying so hard to reach them, and soon I was marching back and forth in front of a bank and wondering whether the world might end before the next chapter of my dissertation came due.

Somewhere between the dream and waking up, Karen and I got married.

"He smells money," I said, sucking in my gut to squeeze past her ladder on my fifth pass through the hallway. "Ennis, I mean. But for some reason, he can't get to it without my help. Otherwise, why would he have called?"

"You're being paranoid," Karen said. "Pick up a scraper and make yourself useful."

"Paranoid?" I said. "You obviously don't know these people."

"I know enough," Karen said. "And I know you, and I know that you have a tendency to blow things out of proportion."

"Is that what you think? That I'm blowing things out of proportion?"

"I think you need to take a breath," Karen said. "Pick up a scraper. Lose yourself in the work. It'll give you some perspective."

I picked up a scraper from the pile of tools on the worn and faded carpet. I pressed the blade to the wallpaper and leaned into it. A three-inch gash appeared in front of me, and a wrinkled, yellow strip came away from the wall.

"See?" Karen asked. "I'll bet you're feeling better already."

"Much," I said, and put down the scraper to resume my pacing. "The problem is that I don't know what I agreed to."

"You didn't agree to anything," Karen said. "Except maybe lunch on Friday."

"Lunch," I said, squeezing past the stepladder once again. "That's how they get you. It starts with lunch, and soon you're agreeing to everything they say."

"You make it sound like a cult," Karen said.

"A cult," I said, turning on my heel and shaking a finger. "That's exactly what I'm dealing with. Propaganda. Brainwashing. Indoctrination. You just watch. On Friday, I'll come home, and I'll be a different person. They know which buttons to push. They know how to get me to do what they want. They know because they made me who I am."

"Then don't go," Karen said.

"I have to go," I said. "That's part of the program."

"Then there's really no point in obsessing over it, is there?"

"I'm not obsessing," I said.

To prove it I squeezed past Karen's stepladder one last time, picked up the scraper, and went back to work on the wallpaper. This was about Billy, I reminded myself as the blade bit into the wall. I was working with the Academy because his mother said that he loved the place. I was meeting with Ennis out of deference to his good name. I was honoring his memory because I should have been a better friend while he was still alive.

I was selling my soul to save it.

On a good day, Neil's commute was two hours long. That Friday, however, was not a good day, and he let me know it as I shoved my giant dollar sign into the backseat of his car. An overturned tractor-trailer had snarled traffic on I-95 for the better part of the morning, so by the time he got to work, he was already late for lunch. In practical terms, this meant that he'd have to stay at his desk until eight or nine that night, depending on how late our meeting with Ennis ran, or he could spread the hours out over the course of the following week. Either way, it meant less time at home and more time at his desk, all because some moron in a tractor-trailer took a turn too quickly.

And, Neil failed to add, because some moron dressed like a giant dollar sign had committed him to a lunchtime meeting he could have easily gone without. That my costume was shedding tiny flakes of green and gold glitter all over his backseat didn't make matters any better, nor did the fact that I was wearing a pair of lime-green stockings under my cargo shorts. At least the boots made sense, I told myself as I untied the balloons from my wrist and wrestled them to the rear of the car. Or they *would* make sense, anyway, if the morning's weather report proved right and we got the rain we'd been promised.

"Have you thought about working from home?" I asked, pulling the puffy white gloves from my hands as if doing so might offset the effect of the stockings. "Telecommuting. The virtual office. I hear it's the next big thing."

"That'll never work," Neil said. "I need to be in the office. I'm a different man behind a desk—as any stenographer will tell you."

"You have a stenographer?" I asked.

"No," Neil said. "It's a line."

"Right," I said. "Groucho Marx."

"*A Night in Casablanca.*"

"I was about to say that."

"Sure you were," Neil said.

"Just tell me one thing," I said, trying to hide my ignorance by giving Neil the only Marx Brothers line I was reasonably sure of. "Why a duck?"

"Too easy," Neil said. "*The Cocoanuts.* I'm all right. How are you?"

If he objected to my ridiculous choice of footwear, he didn't let on, just like he didn't balk when I told him about Ennis's request for an audience or even when I asked if he'd give me a ride. Instead, he just asked where and when to pick me up—two questions I could answer with relative ease. Everything else about the situation had me stumped.

"What do you think he wants?" Neil asked as we motored toward the highway.

"Ennis? What do you think he wants? More money."

"Yeah, but why us? We've already proven that we're no good at this kind of thing."

"What can I say? Maybe the guy believes in second chances."

"Guilt is more like it," Neil said. "We failed him once, so now we'll need to prove ourselves."

"What? Redemption?"

"It worked at the Academy."

"Yeah, but we're adults now."

Neil glanced at my boots and then at the balloons in his rearview mirror, but he didn't say a word. Elvis Costello was singing on the radio. Neil cranked the volume and lowered his windows. As the world flew by at sixty miles per hour, we became children again—or pretended to, at any rate—belting out song lyrics with the wind whipping all around us. It wasn't freedom, exactly, but a small part of me wondered what would happen if Neil laid a heavy foot on the gas and kept going—past the Academy, through the city, over the Delaware, and straight out to the Jersey shore. Could we have a do-over, I wondered? Could we win back the infinite possibility of childhood? If we drove fast enough and played our music loud enough, could we ever outrun the ghost of Billy Chin?

But the sky was already turning gray, the music proving just a little too loud. By the time we were bouncing along the narrow, broken streets that led to the Academy, Neil had raised the windows and turned down his stereo as if suddenly remembering that he was an adult now and that adults had to at least pretend to prefer the staid to the stimulating, prudence to risk, comfort to danger.

BACK WHEN I was a junior, I fell asleep on the bus one morning, and by the time I woke up, the Academy was six stops behind me. It was as far into the neighborhood as I'd ever been, and when I got off the bus, a little girl started chasing me, singing *white, white, white, white, white, white honky* as I ran to school. Less than a block from my destination, I crashed into a homeless man's grocery cart, spilling its contents across the sidewalk and eliciting a string of expletives from its owner.

Apologizing profusely as the little girl laughed at me from across the street, I offered the man my last five dollars, which he took, but not without wrapping his hand around mine and refusing to let go. He was touched by God, he said, and he had the power to heal me. The man was bald, his hands were sticky, and the rattle in his chest sounded like a Geiger counter. The only way to make him let go of me was to promise to repent, so I did, then ran the last fifty yards to school where I rolled up my sleeves and scrubbed the length of my forearm over the sink in the men's room. I was still scrubbing when I heard a toilet flush and saw Frank Dearborn appear in the mirror behind me.

"Fooling around with the natives, Schwartz?"

"Oh," I said, trying to laugh it off. "You saw that."

"The kid was a little young for you, don't you think?" Frank checked himself out in the mirror next to mine. "And somehow I doubt she's one of the chosen. What would your mother say if you brought home a *goy*?"

"I told you before, Frank—"

"And a child, no less," he said, aping Jackie Mason. "And not just a child, but a—what's the word I'm looking for Schwartz? The word your people use for—you know—African Americans?"

I knew the answer but didn't want to say it.

"Wait a second," Frank said, snapping his fingers. "It's on the tip of my tongue."

"*Schwartzer*," I said to myself as he spoke the word aloud.

"Well, that explains a lot," Frank said. "And, really, who am I to judge? If that kind of thing makes you happy, Schwartz, then *mazel tov*, I say."

He slapped me on the back and left me to my scrubbing.

I told Neil all of this if only to bridge the silence between us as the Academy came into view—a massive, walled-in fortress sitting tight among the crumbling homes of the neighborhood it had called home for well over a century. Although surrounding enclaves were slowly giving way to gentrification, the Academy had, in recent years, taken advantage of the fact that the homes on the block immediately to the north were virtually unlivable. Demolition had begun the previous December, and by the time Neil and I arrived on the scene for our audience with Ennis, the homes were gone. In their place lay a fenced-in parking lot shaded by baby sycamores.

"Say what you want about Ennis," Neil said as a security guard waved us into the lot from his air-conditioned booth. "But the guy's doing a hell of a job fixing the place up."

Neil parked his Pontiac between an Audi and a Lexus and told me to be careful when I opened my door. The last thing he needed, he said, was a lawsuit from some seventeen-year-old trust-fund baby for scratching the finish on his car.

Across the street, the Church of Saint Leonard stood tall behind the gray stone walls that surrounded the Academy. Just like we called the Academy *the Academy*, we referred to the Church of Saint Leonard simply as *the Church*, as if there were no other. Back when Neil and I were students, there was talk, however idle, of tearing the whole thing down because it had fallen into such disrepair that a renovation would cost more than the building was worth; but under Ennis's leadership, the alumni association had raised enough money to replace the roof, chase the pigeons out of the steeple, and restore the building's marble façade to the gleaming glory of its heyday.

Passing beneath the stone archway that led to the Academy's courtyard was like stepping back in time and halfway across the world to a filmmaker's notion of what the renaissance might have looked like if it had been designed with teenage boys in mind. To the left stood the newly restored Church with its towering white columns, brass doors, and polished marble steps. Straight ahead, the Academy appeared to recline in ageless, stolid rectitude, an unassailable stone bastion of learning and tradition. Between the two was the faculty parking lot, where even the cars appeared to come from an earlier century, particularly compared to the newer makes and models parked in the student lot across the street.

Inside, teenage boys swarmed all around us in a frenzy of bad skin, rumpled sport coats, and loose neckties, and the stench of puberty hung in the air like an unsavory stew of mushrooms, onions, and gym socks.

"The human body takes many strange forms," Neil said, wading through the sea of pimply teens. "Can you believe this used to be us?"

"You, maybe," I said. "But I was never this young."

A black and white photo of the freshman class was tacked to the bulletin board outside the cafeteria. There were no goofy faces in the bunch, just a small regiment of serious boys scowling at the camera and pretending to be men.

AFTER CHECKING in with the registrar, Neil and I climbed two flights of steps and followed a narrow hallway to the byzantine suite of offices that once belonged to the faculty, but which Ennis had, over the years, commandeered as his efforts at raising money took on monstrously successful dimensions. Raising a finger when his secretary showed us to his office door, Ennis wrapped up a telephone conversation and told us to please have a seat.

The carpet was a deep shade of red, and the walls were lined with books: *Siddhartha, Man's Search for Meaning, Twilight of the Idols,* and dozens of others with equally intimidating titles. Was Ennis a closet philosopher, I wondered, or were the volumes mere props pilfered from the Academy library to make him look smarter than he really was?

"Gentlemen," he said as Neil and I sank into a pair of soft, leather easy chairs. "I wish we could be meeting under better circumstances, but it's always good to see a pair of familiar faces."

Ennis's eyes fell on my rubber boots and green stockings, but when I opened my mouth to explain, he looked away as if he'd just caught me listening to a Barry Manilow record or touching myself in a toilet stall. Some things were better left unmentioned, his sudden, awkward silence said as a small refrigerator hummed under his minibar.

"As I was explaining to Charley the other day," Ennis continued, focusing his attention on Neil so as not, I supposed, to concern himself with my fashion sense, "we have a few options in terms of—remembering—your friend most effectively."

"Billy," I said. "Can we please use his name? His name was Billy."

"By all means," Ennis said. "We want to remember Billy as he was. Kind, loyal, generous. A true scholar and a man for others. A paragon of Noblac ideals, if you will. Did you see the Church on your way in?"

"It was hard to miss," Neil said.

"That was my first campaign," Ennis said. "I hate to use the word *capitalize*, but Brother Timothy's passing made the project feasible—at least in terms of economics. You remember Brother Timothy, don't you?"

"Sure," I said. "Brown robe, thick glasses. A bit of a donkey fetish."

Neil coughed into his fist. Ennis looked sideways at me, then went on with his speech.

"As tragic as it was, Brother Timothy's passing gave our community a sense of focus. It allowed us to reflect upon the larger ideals of the Noblac order and how central they are to all of our lives. It gave us an opportunity to remember what service, scholarship, and loyalty mean to everyone who's ever been touched by the Academy in one way or another."

"Or touched by Brother Timothy," I said.

"Death has a way of drawing people together," Ennis said, ignoring me completely. "A way of reminding us of the values we share. This death, the death of your friend—of Billy—has the potential to bring a sizable portion of your class back into the fold. A brief letter to inform everyone of his passing. A memorial service here at the school. Maybe a few words about his friendship and what it meant to you. I'm sure you can see how such gestures might be effective in helping us reach our larger goal."

"Which is?" Neil said.

"Preserving a way of life," Ennis said as if this much were self-evident. "Upholding the time-honored values of the Noblac order. Molding the boys of today into the leaders of tomorrow."

"So we're talking about money," I said.

"We're talking about the greater good," Ennis said.

Somewhere between *greater* and *good*, my cell phone went off and a gospel choir started to serenade us with the theme from *The Jeffersons*. Though I tried to pretend that it wasn't *my* phone informing us that we were moving on up to the East Side, it was pretty clear by the time the choir got to the deluxe apartment in the sky that the tune was coming from the left pocket of my cargo shorts. Privately cursing Anthony Gambacorta for screwing with my ringtone and (after I checked to see who was calling) Sean Sullivan for trying, more than likely, to sell me a Volkswagen at such an inopportune moment, I switched off the phone and looked up just in time to see the devil himself standing in the doorway.

"Here's our man," Ennis said, rising from his desk. "You boys remember Frank Dearborn, don't you?"

The air went out of me as Ennis put an arm around Frank's shoulders and ushered him into the room. He had the same Abercrombie & Fitch good looks I remembered from high school. The same swagger, too. His only flaw, if you could even call it that, was still his crooked nose. Sure, he looked a little older, but not the way Neil and I looked older—with our already receding hairlines and the paunch of a few too many beers creeping slowly over our guts. For

Frank, growing older meant nothing more than the finest of wrinkles in the corners of his eyes when he smiled and shook our hands. For Frank, growing older meant a deeper tan and a sharper suit. For Frank, growing older meant that he was still, in every way, our social better.

"Jesus, guys," Frank said, apparently in reference to Billy. "I still can't believe it. What do you think happened?"

What do I think happened? I wanted to scream. You can't be serious! People like you happened, Frank. Day in, day out, the butt of all your jokes. The poor guy couldn't take it anymore. The only miracle is that it didn't happen sooner.

"I keep thinking about how much fun we used to have," Frank said. "All those songs? *Billy Chin is not my lover.* God, I can't even begin."

"I know what you mean," Neil said as I held my tongue.

"And the time he found the kittens in bio lab?"

"That's right," Ennis said. "You boys were in my class together."

"I already told you that," I said. "Remember? On the phone?"

"We used to laugh so much," Frank said as if I weren't in the room. "I still can't believe he's gone."

"*I'm* the one who found the kittens," I said, inexplicably intent on setting the record straight. "That was *me*."

"But it was Billy's cat," Frank said. "Right?"

"It was *our* cat," I said. "Billy was my lab partner."

"Time does have a tendency to make a blur of things," Ennis said. "For better or for worse."

"Are you kidding?" I asked, looking to Neil for even a modicum of support. "I remember like it was yesterday. You asked me what I was doing, and I said I was cutting open the cat's scrotal sack. Then you told the class to come and watch, and when I cut it open, the kittens popped out."

"That's right!" Frank shouted. "They popped out and Ennis asked if your scrotum was full of kittens."

"Something like that," I said, suddenly wishing I'd left well enough alone. "Billy tried to warn me."

"Fun times," Frank said wistfully. "But like they say, you can't live in the past, right?"

Screw you, Frank, I thought as Ennis went to the minibar and asked the bastard if he wanted his regular drink. *I can live anywhere I want—including the past.*

Frank's job, Ennis explained, was to help me and Neil with the letter. And, of course, with planning Billy's memorial service. There were, after all, a lot of details to consider—what to serve, how big a crowd to invite, whether or not to involve the press. In short, Frank was there to make sure we got the most bang for the Academy's buck.

"I think we can handle it on our own," I said.

"No worries, gentlemen," Ennis insisted. "Think of Frank as part of the team. He was doing some consulting for us a while back when I figured out that it was cheaper to hire him full time. Publicity and marketing, mainly. The man's a wizard when it comes to finding the right words."

"What can I say?" Frank said, taking the drink from Ennis. "Working for the Academy is my *mitzvah*. Know what I mean, Schwartz?"

"This letter," Neil said before I could answer. "It's what? An invitation to the memorial service?"

"More or less," Ennis explained. "You can leave the details to Frank. All we really need is for you and Schwartz to sign off on it."

"It really isn't a big deal," Frank said. "We'll mention Billy's passing and how much the Academy meant to him. We'll talk about the new cafeteria, the new gym, the new swimming pool. Drop a few hints about how much money it all cost. With any luck, we'll get some checks in the mail and a few bodies in the door on the day of the service. The real trick is to keep things light and not dwell too much on the negative aspects of the situation."

Frank stirred his drink with his finger.

"Keep things light?" I said. "Billy killed himself."

"That's one story," Ennis said. "But it's not the only one."

"You're saying he didn't?"

"I'm saying there's a difference between the forest and the trees."

"Ideally, we try to avoid specifics in cases like this," Frank added. "Only because they detract from the larger message. But like Phil said, leave the letter to me. All we need from you guys are a couple of signatures and your blessing."

"Our blessing?" I said.

"A letter from me is one thing," Frank said. "But a letter from you guys?"

"But it won't be from us," I said. "It'll be from you."

"In spirit, the letter will be from all of us," Ennis said. "But with your imprimatur—"

"Our imprimatur?" I asked.

"It means endorsement," Frank said. "Your seal of approval."

"I know what the word means," I shouted, struggling to rise from my deep, soft chair with an air of authority. "I just don't know why—"

"We'll do what we can," Neil said quietly. "Whatever you need, just let us know."

I turned and glared at him.

"We understand that it's a tragic situation," Ennis said, stepping forward and turning out his hand to indicate that our audience had reached its end. "But it's times like these that bring out the best in all of us."

"Exactly," Frank said, raising his glass in our direction as Ennis made a less than subtle gesture toward the door. "Grace under pressure."

I choked back my rage as Neil thanked Ennis for his time and told Frank that it was great to see him again. Gradually herding us out of his office, Ennis said that Frank would be in touch as soon as he had a draft of the letter. We could feel free to tweak it a little to make it sound more personal, Frank added, calling after us from inside the office, but in the meantime Neil and I could give some thought to the kinds of refreshments we wanted for the memorial service—and if either of us was up for it, to come up with a few nice words about Billy.

"So," Neil said as Ennis closed his door behind us and our footsteps echoed down the cold, stone stairwell that led to the ground floor. "Frank Dearborn."

"Yeah," I said, shaking my head in disbelief. "Frank Dearborn."

Beyond that, there was nothing more to say.

❧ CHAPTER EIGHT ❧

A soft rain had begun to fall as Neil turned out of the Academy parking lot and onto the broken street. His windshield wipers slapped a steady beat as we passed the row homes, pawnshops, taverns, bus stops, liquor stores, churches, supermarkets, and gas stations that slumped shoulder to shoulder in various states of disrepair along the narrow wrecked roads of North Philadelphia. Some of the houses were undergoing reconstruction, but most were crumbling to the ground. Halfway down a block, we'd see a gap in the row, like a missing tooth in an ugly, brown smile. The vacant space would be overrun with weeds and stray cats, and the imprint of the fallen home would still be visible on the flanks of its neighbors—where the floorboards had been, the walls and the staircase. People used to live in these spaces, I thought to myself. They used to sit down to dinner and talk about their days or lie awake at night and wonder how to make ends meet. They had holidays here. First dates and clandestine meetings. They talked and loved and fought and lived, and now they were gone. Ghosts. Memories. Dust.

"I told you we shouldn't have come through Australia," Neil said, doing Groucho once again as his Pontiac bumped along Girard Avenue. "You know it's all ripped up. We should have gone straight up Lincoln Boulevard."

"I don't know," I said, assuming it was yet another cue to spit out the wrong title of a Marx Brothers movie.

"Take a guess," Neil said.

"Do I have to?"

"Here's a hint: Last night I shot an elephant in my pajamas. How he got in my pajamas, I'll never know."

"I really don't feel like it."

"Not even close," Neil said. "But thanks for playing just the same."

"Can you at least try to be serious for once?"

"Me?" Neil said. "I'm not the one with *The Jeffersons* ringtone. How'd that get on your phone anyway?"

"Anthony did it," I said. "It was a birthday present."

"And you haven't thought about changing it?"

"Of course I've thought about changing it," I said. "But there's a principle involved."

"Right," Neil said. "A principle."

We crossed the Schuylkill at 34th Street and passed the zoo where street vendors were still out, hawking soft pretzels and inflatable superheroes despite the rain.

"You could have at least said something back there," I said. "All that bullshit about Noblac ideals and bringing more alums back into the fold?"

"What was I supposed to say?"

"I don't know," I said. "How about that Frank's an asshole? How about that Ennis could go to hell? How about that we weren't going to sign their stupid letter? That would have been a nice start."

"What good would it have done, Charley?"

"We're talking about Billy," I said. "We're talking about his memory. What do you mean what good would it have done?"

"They're doing this with or without us," Neil said. "And in the end, who knows? Maybe they're right. At least this way, something good comes of it."

"Of Billy's suicide?" I said.

"Yes," Neil said. "Of Billy's suicide."

"So we just, what? Roll over and take it?"

"We make the best of it," Neil said as I realized that we missed the on-ramp for I-76. "I haven't mentioned this to anyone, but my father isn't doing so well."

"Is it his heart again?" I asked.

"No," Neil said. "Alzheimer's."

I didn't know what to say.

I never know what to say.

Neil's dad printed forms for a living, documentation and paperwork for banks and small businesses. *Name, Date, Social Security Number,* I thought to myself. *Fill in the blank. Check all that apply. Press firmly with ballpoint pen: __I'm sorry your father is sick. __I'm sorry he'll forget your name. __I'm sorry you'll watch him fade over time. __I'm sorry he'll look at your children one day and smile blandly like my grandmother used to as he wonders who they are and why they're hugging him, and I'm sorry they'll never know how funny he was, how witty, how smart, how full of life.*

__I'll never forget the summer after college when the world was still big and full of possibility, how you'd call me at work and say let's go to the shore, and I'd grab a fresh shirt, and we'd meet up for pizza and beer and talk about everything life had in store for us.

__And I'll always remember the night a girl cut her toe on a broken bottle and her boyfriend threw a punch at the guy who dropped it, and a table turned over and the whole place exploded, and the cops burst in wearing gas masks and riot gear as we slipped out a side door with a couple of Asian women who spoke twelve words of English between them and asked for a ride back to Wildwood where they were living with their cousins; one had to be fifty, and the other was her mother, and they were both wearing skintight sequin dresses, and when we pulled up to a motel after a thousand wrong turns, ten guys with mustaches and butterfly knives swarmed around the car as the women stepped out, and they eyed us up and down, flicking their knives and lighting unfiltered cigarettes as they tried to decide how to dispose of our bodies

*until one of the girls said something in a language we didn't
know and the men started laughing and slapping the hood
of your car, the roof, and the windshield, and the younger
woman leaned in as if to kiss you goodnight and said, "Don't
worry, big boy, I tell them you candyass homo couple big-
time," and we both nodded and said goodnight as you threw
the car into gear and peeled out of the parking lot in a cloud
of exhaust fumes and burning rubber, a small army of Asian
men laughing their asses off in your rearview mirror as we
vowed to never breathe a word of the incident to anyone.*

*___And now your father's sick, and I wish I had the words
to make sense of everything I want to tell you.*

NEIL FOUND a cramped pizzeria where a man in an apron
stood behind the counter and tossed dough in the air. We
ordered a medium pie and two iced teas and sat in a booth
by a window where flies beat their wings in vain against the
glass. We ate and talked. We sipped our drinks and ordered
refills. Watching from a distance, a stranger might get the
impression that Neil was my accountant or my insurance
agent or maybe even a social worker assigned to deal with a
mentally challenged adult with a penchant for rubber boots
and brightly colored stockings. Up close, the impression I
got was more or less the same.

This was my friend, I thought to myself as Neil filled me
in on the details of his father's illness: he was still in the
early stages, still recognized faces, was starting on Raza-
dyne, but the look of almost perpetual confusion and frustration on his face said that he wasn't the man he used
to be. There was a time when Neil and I talked all the
time, when no secret was too great, no dream too wild. Now
this was what passed for our relationship—exchanging the
digest versions of each other's lives in a fiberglass booth at
some dirty, run-down pizza place.

"And the hits keep coming," Neil said. "Madeline got a job."

"That's great," I said. "Isn't it?"

Neil's head bobbed from side to side. "It's in Baltimore."

It wasn't much further than where she was already going to school, Neil said, but living in Delaware was too much for them—not the state so much, but splitting their lives between two cities.

"Two hours each day," he said. "And for Madeline, it's worse. The good news is I can waive into DC, so the bar exam won't be an issue."

I wasn't sure what this meant, but I smiled and nodded anyway.

"My mother's a wreck," Neil said. "She thinks we're abandoning her and my dad in their time of need."

"At least you'll get Packer out of your hair," I said.

"*That* guy," Neil said. "You wouldn't believe half the shit he does. He called me at work the other day and asked if I could drive him to Conshohocken for a haircut."

"That was me," I said.

Neil laughed, so I laughed, too, but if I wanted to be honest with myself, I had to admit that calling him away from his job to pull me out of the mud suggested that I was at least a little clingy, if not entirely helpless.

"That was different," Neil said. "You wanted to tell me about Billy. All Greg ever wants is a free ride and a haircut—though this time around it's a ride to the hospital."

"Is he sick?" I asked.

"No," Neil said. "He wants an epidural."

"No kidding," I said. "Who's the father?"

"It has something to do with his back and this girl he's meeting in Chicago. He sent her a picture, by the way."

"And it didn't scare her off?"

"It was a picture of me."

"Creepy," I said. "Why do you bother?"

"I don't know," Neil said. "I've been thinking about Billy lately. Maybe with Greg we can make a difference."

"I know what you mean," I said. "I still feel—I wish we'd done something. I wish *I'd* done something. Said something, even."

"You can't think like that," Neil said. "It'll make you crazy."

"Too late," I said. "Do you feel like going for a ride?"

"I have to get back to work," Neil said.

"Me too, but there's something I need to see."

Neil rolled his eyes by way of protest, but a mischievous grin spread across his face at the thought, I guessed, of skipping work for one last romp with his best friend before he moved.

"Call Dwayne," I said. "It's in his neck of the woods."

DWAYNE LIVED alone in a three-bedroom twin on the outer fringes of Philadelphia. As a civil servant, he was bound by law to live within city limits, but as a human being, it was the last place on Earth he wanted to live. The solution most civil servants found to this dilemma was to take up residence in the northernmost part of the city—north of North Philly and west of the Northeast in neighborhoods like Chestnut Hill, Manayunk, Germantown, and Roxborough—the same part of the city where Billy had grown up.

"Do you know what time it is?" Dwayne asked when we arrived on his doorstep. "I'm working nights this week."

"I told you he'd be cranky," Neil said. "The man needs his beauty rest."

Dwayne stood, unamused, in his doorway, wearing nothing but a tattered brown robe and fuzzy blue slippers. In the two years he'd lived in the house, he only invited us inside once, and that was to move furniture. Since then, he'd painted the walls and had carpets installed, so whenever Neil and I visited, Dwayne stopped us at the door lest we track mud all over the place like a couple of wild animals. Holding up a pizza box, I said we brought lunch, but he only opened his door wide enough to join us on the front steps.

"It's cold," he said, opening the box. "And you took a bite out of it."

"I got hungry," I said. "Listen, we need your help. Can you show us how to get to the Henry Avenue Bridge?"

"No way," Dwayne said. "Bad idea."

Radio towers loomed over his house, red warning lights flashing in the gray, gloomy sky.

"I just want to look," I said.

"Trust me," Dwayne said. "The view is terrible."

"I'm not talking about the view," I said. "I'm talking about closure."

"Closure? Please. Morbid curiosity's more like it."

"Morbid curiosity, then. I want to see it."

"You crossed that bridge to get here," Dwayne said. "Isn't that enough?"

"We did?" Neil said.

"No," I said. "I don't think so."

"Christ," Dwayne said, lifting a cold slice from the box. "Where's the car?"

If I were a considerate friend, I'd have let Dwayne take the front seat, but the part of me that let him squeeze into the back of Neil's Pontiac with my balloons and my giant dollar sign also told me it would be funny to force his knees up to his chest by pushing the passenger seat as far back as it would go. Still in his bathrobe, Dwayne called me an asshole, then grunted directions at Neil between bites of cold pizza.

Dwayne was right, of course. I *was* an asshole and probably still am, but the voice that told me it would be funny to crush Dwayne's knees with the passenger seat also told me that my brand of assholery, if such a thing exists, was the good kind, the kind that let guys like us push each other around and call each other pussies and make jokes about each other's mothers even when they were dead or dying of unspeakable diseases. Crushing Dwayne's knees was like breaking his balls, I told myself. It said I knew I could fool around with him, knew that deep down he had a good sense of humor, and knew most of all that he could take it. If there was anything four years at the Academy had taught me, it was that the best way to tell my friends I loved them was through torture and abuse. But as we neared the Henry Avenue Bridge, I remembered that the lesson was completely lost on Billy.

The evening commute was hours away, but the avenue was already heavy with traffic as Neil parked his car and we walked the hundred or so yards of tree-lined sidewalk that led to the bridge. If anyone on the force saw him out and about in his bathrobe, Dwayne complained, it could mean his badge. They'd arrest him for indecent exposure or, worse, force him into counseling if the wind happened to blow his robe open at just the right moment.

"Quit complaining," I said. "You had plenty of time to change before we got here."

"Into what?" Dwayne asked. "I haven't done laundry in weeks."

"And this is my fault?"

"Maybe I was planning to do some today."

"I'm sure of it," I said.

"I'm saying *maybe*."

I turned to give Neil a look of contempt for our sartorially challenged friend and realized that we'd lost him somewhere between his car and the bridge.

"Hey, pal!" I shouted when I turned around and spotted him about twenty paces back. "Are you coming or what?"

"You guys go ahead," Neil said. "I'll wait here."

"No way," I said. "We're doing this together."

"I can't, Charley. I'm not good with heights."

"Neither am I, remember?"

"No," Neil said. "I mean it. I'm *really* not good with heights."

"But your honeymoon," I said. "The helicopter. You sent me pictures."

"I bought them from a kid at the airport."

"Whatever," I said. "This is totally different. You drive across bridges all the time."

"Driving's one thing," Neil said. "Walking's another. You'll want me to look down, and I can't do that."

"Nobody wants you to look down," I said. "We're only taking a walk. You need to trust me on this, Neil. It'll be good for you. A chance to say goodbye to Billy on our own terms before all this crap with the Academy gets out of control."

Neil kept his eyes on his feet and followed us to the center of the bridge. It was a slow walk, and the rain had turned to a fine mist. In my mind, I could picture Billy walking ahead of me. If I hurried, I thought, maybe I could catch him. If I matched his footsteps stride for stride, maybe I could place myself in Billy's shoes and make him walk back home. Or if I stood where he stood and saw what he saw and thought what he thought, maybe I could reach back in time and stop him from doing what he did.

From below, the Henry Avenue Bridge looks like an aqueduct—stone arches curving down into massive concrete pilings—but all we could see were the tops of trees and the river coursing through the valley below.

A low concrete wall ran along the edge of the bridge. I laid my hands on it and leaned over.

"This is it," I said, the arches of my feet tingling with fear. "This is where he did it."

"Jesus," Neil said. "Get back from there."

I leaned out a little further. The drop had to be at least two hundred feet.

"He woke up one day, and that was it," I said. "He got dressed, walked out the door and headed straight for this bridge."

I hoisted myself up onto the wall. It was waist-high and as accommodating as a park bench as I swung my legs over the edge, one then the other, and let them dangle. Looking out over the trees, I could feel the tingle in my feet spreading to my knees. Neil looked away. Dwayne told me to cut it out. I could feel Billy sitting next to me. When I turned my head, I could almost see him.

"Come and look," I said.

"For Christ's sake," Dwayne said. "Would you get down from there?"

"This was the last thing Billy saw," I said.

"He was in a bad place."

"Fuck a bad place," I said. "He was the smartest guy I knew."

I leaned forward, and the tingle spread to my elbows and wrists. My breath was shallow. My stomach was turning. It would be so easy, I thought. Not that I wanted to. Not that I was considering it. But I could see the attraction—a gesture so ordinary, like rising from a seat or stepping off a curb.

"Come look," I said.

"We look, you come down," Dwayne said. "That's the deal, okay?"

"Absolutely."

Dwayne took a step forward and peered over the edge.

"Neil?" I said.

"You said I wouldn't have to."

"You don't, but it'll be good for you."

He inched toward the wall. He laid his hands on the concrete. He leaned over the edge.

"Jesus," he said, and sank to his knees.

"Now come on down," Dwayne said. "That was the deal."

"I can't," I said.

"Quit fooling around."

"I'm serious," I said. "I can't move my legs."

"Come on," Dwayne said. "Just swing around. One leg and then the other."

I turned my head, but Billy was gone. I couldn't see him, couldn't feel his presence, couldn't even remember his face. He was there one second and gone the next. Down below were the tops of trees. Down below was the river. Down below was the choice he made, and deep inside I hated him for it.

"Fucking asshole," I croaked. "Why'd he do it?"

"You're the fucking asshole," Dwayne said, looping a long, bony arm across my chest and dragging me backwards to safety. "Not Billy."

My face was red. My throat was tight. I wanted Dwayne to punch me, to really let me have it for always treating him like shit, to beat the hell out of me for always dragging him down, to completely lay me out for always turning everything into a joke, but instead he just helped Neil back onto his feet and walked away in silence as cars and trucks whipped past us on their way over the bridge. Overhead, the clouds grew heavy, and the red lights of the radio towers behind Dwayne's house pulsed slow and steady in the darkening afternoon sky.

✎ CHAPTER NINE ✎

When Neil dropped me off at the bank, Sue was standing under the drive-thru canopy to shelter herself from the rain as she smoked a cigarette. We'd made eye contact as Neil pulled into the parking lot, so there was no point in telling him to keep driving. Not that he would have listened—I could tell he was pretty pissed at me for the stunt I'd just pulled on the bridge. Besides, he was already so late for work that there was no real point in showing up at all. At best, he'd lose a sick day. At worst, he'd be written up for dereliction of duty or something equally onerous. That was the thing about having a real job, Neil said, breaking the tense silence between us to remind me that only one of us had fully crossed over into adulthood. You couldn't just ditch work for the hell of it. You had to show up every day, whether you wanted to or not.

I could have put up a fight if I wanted to—could have insisted that I did, in fact, have a real job with real consequences and all the other grown-up shit Neil was talking about—but the oversized dollar sign shedding glitter on his backseat made winning the argument an unlikely prospect. Instead of arguing, I mumbled an apology as I wrestled the ridiculous costume out of his car, and I asked if he was still up for helping me write the invitation to Billy's memorial service.

"I'm sure Frank can handle it," Neil said, barely glancing over his shoulder to respond.

"That isn't the point," I said. "I don't want him in charge of this. Or Ennis, either. This is ours. I want it to be ours."

"Okay," Neil said. "But no fucking around this time. I mean it."

"Right," I said. "No fucking around."

I closed the door and tapped on the roof of Neil's car by way of goodbye. He was barely out of the parking lot when I turned around to find myself toe to toe with my supervisor. The rain was still falling, and she didn't have an umbrella, so I guessed that whatever she had to tell me was worth ruining what had to be her best off-white ruffled blouse. I guessed, in other words, that I was about to be fired.

"What's going on?" she asked. "Where have you been?"

"Sorry," I said. "It was an emergency."

"Unless someone's dead, I don't want to hear it."

"Someone *is* dead," I said. "A friend of mine killed himself."

Had there been any color in Sue's face, it would have drained away right then and there. Her mouth hung open, silent and uncertain, for a full minute as her brain tried to decide whether or not I was telling the truth.

"I'm sorry," she eventually said, reaching out to touch my forearm.

"Yeah, well."

"Really, Charley, take the rest of the day off."

It was the first time that Sue had ever used my name— at least that I noticed, anyway—and hearing it made me want to cry. Not my name, so much, but the way she said it, the way she was so willing to believe what I told her. And even though it was true, even though a friend of mine had, in fact, killed himself, I felt sick to my stomach over saying it, over using Billy's death to hang on to the dumbest job I'd ever had in my life.

"Yeah," I said. "I think that would be a good idea."

"Charley?" Sue said as I started toward my car. "We still need to talk, okay?"

"Talk?" I said.

"You're up for a performance review. We need to talk about the work you've been doing."

"Right," I said. "Work."

"But it can wait," she said. "It can so totally wait."

"Thanks," I said. "Totally."

⚭⋀⚭

I came home to walls of bare, jaundiced plaster and furniture draped in old bed sheets. On Thursday, Karen and I had tried to paint the walls of the dining room only to watch the paint bead up as soon as it came into contact with the plaster. Apparently this meant that there was still glue on the walls, and that we still had countless hours of scrubbing and scraping ahead of us before we could try once more to paint the walls and make the house our own.

If I had any sense at all, I'd have started scrubbing long before Karen got home, but I opted instead for pulling away the lavender sheet that covered our television and catching the end of a soap opera, a vice I'd picked up in the early days of grad school. Initially, I'd attributed my fascination with the constant rise and fall of convoluted love affairs to a dutiful urge to immerse myself in the tropes and themes of lowbrow American culture; but in reality watching soap operas was oddly comforting. There was a certain logic to the genre that was hard to resist, a constant reassurance that as tangled and hopeless as circumstances were bound to become, things would always even out in the end.

Plus the women were hot.

Aside from that, what made me reach for the remote almost as soon as I'd walked in the door was the eternal prospect of characters returning from the dead. A year earlier, I'd seen a teenager die in a fire only to come back without any memory of his former life. Not long after that, an evil millionaire was found frozen alive in Antarctica after being presumed dead for over a decade. Then there was the supermodel who drove her car off a cliff only to be rescued, it was revealed three months later, by a megalo-maniac arms dealer.

Given the apparent propensity for the dead to return to life on all my favorite soaps, it wasn't so crazy for me to lose myself, if only for a little while, in the fantasy that maybe there'd been a mistake, that maybe Billy wasn't dead. Yes, there'd been a suicide, I allowed myself to think, but it wasn't him. The old man who identified the body was wrong—he had to be. Someone else had jumped—some poor, tortured soul I'd never met. But Billy had just gone away for a while and forgotten to tell everyone. Someday soon, he'd come back healthy and strong and full of stories about his travels—how he'd fallen in and out of love with a Russian spy, how he'd foiled a hijacking plot off the coast of Belize, how he'd nearly lost an eye in a barroom brawl when a ninety-year-old woman with a hook for a hand took a swipe at his face. In fact, I thought wistfully, still lost in the soap opera logic of denial, it wasn't inconceivable that Billy was already back in town and waiting for the right time to call.

Then the telephone rang, and I sprang from the sofa, afraid I'd been caught dreaming impossible, childish dreams.

"Charley Schwartz?" a gravelly voice asked when I picked up the phone.

"Yes?" I said as if I weren't sure.

"Joe Viola," the voice said. "Saint Leonard's Academy. I'm calling about this Bobby Chang thing."

"Chin," I said. "His name was Billy Chin."

"That's the one. Were you thinking doughnuts or crudités?"

"I'm not sure," I said. "Doughnuts or—?"

"Crudités. Your buddy Frank suggested egg rolls, but that runs into money."

"He's not my buddy," I said.

"In any case, he said you're the point man on this one, so it's entirely up to you."

"Frank Dearborn is *not* my buddy," I repeated. "You need to understand that."

"So nix the egg rolls."

"Yeah," I said. "Nix the egg rolls. Nix everything Frank tells you."

"That leaves us with doughnuts and crudités."

"Fine," I said. "Doughnuts and crudités."

"You want both?"

"Why?" I said. "Is that wrong?"

"Usually it's one or the other."

"Damn," I said. "How soon do you need an answer?"

"The sooner the better," the voice said. "We're on a tight schedule with this thing."

"How tight?" I said.

"Three weeks," the voice said. "Give or take a few days."

"Bastards," I muttered. "I'll call you right back."

But I never called back. Instead, I paced the living room, boiling with rage at Frank for commandeering Billy's memorial service and leaving me to deal with shit that didn't matter. Doughnuts? Crudités? How was I supposed to know? I wouldn't know a crudité if I choked on one.

When Karen came home from work, I told her in fits and starts about my meeting at the Academy, about Ennis and Frank and how they were suddenly lifelong pals, about their plans for Billy's memorial service and how Ennis wanted me and Neil to sign a letter inviting everyone to attend or, failing that, to at least send a check. I was about to mention the call from Joe Viola and my subsequent dilemma over whether to serve doughnuts or crudités at the service when Karen interrupted my diatribe to ask if I was okay.

"Of course I'm okay," I said as Karen hefted a thick stack of term papers from her schoolbag and laid them on the kitchen table. "I'm just telling you about my day."

"Telling me would be fine," Karen said. "This feels more like a rant."

"A rant?" I said. "Really? You think I'm ranting?"

"I think you seem a little wound up."

"No," I said. "I'm fine."

"You're sure about that?"

"Yeah," I said. "Absolutely. Grade your papers. We'll talk over dinner."

We didn't exactly talk over dinner. Instead, I sighed and grunted and made a lot of aggrieved noises with my upper respiratory system, while I wondered whether or not the steamed carrots and broccoli on the plate in front of me might be considered crudités by those in the know. Meanwhile, the fact that I *wasn't* among those in the know—that I didn't have *any* idea what crudités were—was beginning to get to me, so I nodded on occasion as Karen spoke and supplemented my repertoire of grunts and groans with a bare minimum of noncommittal verbal responses based less on the content of our conversation than on my wife's tone of voice. If she noticed I was out of sorts, she didn't let on—at least, not until bedtime as I was pacing our narrow, unfinished hallway and shoving my toothbrush in and out of my mouth, the issue of whether to serve doughnuts or crudités at Billy's memorial service gathering force in my head and twisting me up inside.

"Let's try it for real this time," Karen said. "What's going on?"

"Nothing," I said, spitting toothpaste into the bathroom sink. "By the way, what the fuck are crudités?"

"Excuse me?"

"You heard me. What the fuck are crudités?"

"So, what? We're dropping f-bombs now?"

"Yeah," I said. "We're dropping fucking f-bombs. Do you know what crudités are or not?"

"They're like canapés," Karen said. "But without the bread. In much the same way that the man I married is like you but without the attitude."

"Attitude?" I said. "What are you talking about? I just want to know what crudités are."

"Vegetables, Charley. What's bothering you?"

"Nothing," I said. "Everything's fine."

"That's funny. Because in my experience, people who are fine don't lose their shit when they hear a new word."

"I didn't—"

"You did, Charley. And you are. You're losing your shit because you don't know what crudités are. Now tell me what's wrong."

I squeezed some more toothpaste onto my toothbrush and shoved it back into my mouth before realizing that I'd already finished brushing my teeth.

"Damn," I said, spitting into the sink again. "Fuck. Fuck, fuck, fuck."

"Charley!" Karen said. "For Christ's sake, would you tell me what's going on?"

"It's nothing," I said. "It's Neil. He's moving."

"That isn't nothing," Karen said. "He's your best friend."

"I know. I just—"

"What?"

"I don't know," I said.

Karen laid a hand on my shoulder, and when I pulled away from her, she reached for me again and made me look her in the eye. I tried to look away, but she moved her hand from my shoulder to my neck and pulled me closer.

"It's all happening so fast," I said. "Billy. Neil. Why do things have to change?"

"You want to work at the bank forever?" Karen asked.

I smiled—not only because Karen was kind enough to use her favorite euphemism for my job, but also because a small part of me would have been content to walk back and forth on the hot, wet lawn in front of the bank until the end of time if it meant that I could keep the world from changing, keep my friends close by, keep everyone I knew safe and happy.

"You're right," I said. "That would be ridiculous."

"I've been letting you slide, Charley," Karen said. "Mainly because of Billy, but at some point it has to stop."

"It will," I said. "When this is all over, I promise."

"And what is 'this' exactly?" Karen asked.

I shrugged my shoulders and let out a sigh. When we got into bed and turned out the lights, I could feel the hard and soft contours of Karen's body against mine. Shoulder blades and elbows. Skull, spine, and ribs. The warm curve of her bottom. The rise and fall of her chest as she breathed. Closing my eyes, I could still see the tops of trees and the river coursing through the valley below as the image of my falling friend fluttered through my mind. Billy's mouth was moving as if he were trying to speak, as if he were trying to tell me something, and for a moment I felt like I was falling with him.

Or not quite with him, I realized, still falling.

But *as* him—headfirst, eyes wide, earth rising skyward.

I was Billy Chin falling, and I was free.

My body jerked. My heart was racing. My hands shook with phantom jitters.

Just nerves, I told myself as Karen snored softly in the darkness, but when I closed my eyes, all I could see were the tops of trees.

❧ CHAPTER TEN ❧

By Saturday morning, the clouds had lifted and the sky was clear. Over breakfast, Karen dropped a prolonged hint about the long day of scrubbing we had ahead of us. What was the best way to remove the paste from our dining room walls, my wife wondered aloud as she pulled a box of cereal down from the cabinet over the stove? Soap and water hadn't done the trick, so maybe it was just a matter of more elbow grease. If we put some serious muscle into it, she mused, pouring cereal for both of us, maybe that would do the trick. Unless I thought we should consider more drastic measures, she said. Chemicals, perhaps. Something caustic, something from the hardware store that would likely cause long-term health problems, but which would, in the short term, fix everything.

I stood in front of the open refrigerator, pretending to look for the milk and then feigning ignorance about everything Karen had just said.

"What was that?" I asked, making a show of finally discovering a half-gallon of milk right under my nose despite the fact that Karen was already seated at the kitchen table with her back to me. "I was looking for the milk."

"The walls," Karen said. "I'm tired of living like this. I want to paint, I want to put all the furniture back in place, and I want to go back to living like normal people. I want my house back, Charley, but right now I feel like it's never going to happen."

"It'll happen," I said. "Don't worry. We'll get it done."

I sat at the table and poured the milk over my cereal.

"The only problem is that I need to work on that invitation today."

"Invitation?" Karen said.

"To Billy's memorial service." I kept my eyes on my cereal. "I promised Phil Ennis that I'd have it done by Monday morning. I thought I told you about this."

"You told me about the crudités."

"Sorry," I said. "There's so much going on. The service is in three weeks, so I need to get this invitation done right away."

"Three weeks?"

"It's the only date they had open."

It wasn't a lie, exactly. It was more of an extrapolation based on the information that Joe Viola had provided.

"Is there anything else you forgot to tell me?" Karen asked.

"No," I said. "That should cover it."

Although I should probably mention that I took a trip to the bridge where Billy Chin killed himself, I thought as I brought a spoonful of bran flakes to my mouth. *Oh, and no big deal here, really, but Dwayne Coleman had to wrestle me to the ground when I got too close to the edge. Other than that, no, I don't think there's anything else I need to tell you.*

After breakfast, I could hear Karen scrubbing away in the dining room as I drummed on a pad of paper with the tip of my pen. For the most part, the page in front of me was blank. *Dear Fellow Alums,* the invitation read in its entirety. Beyond that, I didn't know what to say. For all of my disturbing dreams, my waking thoughts about Billy weren't moving me in one way or the other. In some ways, I felt as if he were still alive, as if I could call him whenever I wanted, but didn't because we were both so busy all the time. Which wasn't much different from how our relationship worked while Billy was still alive.

Crossing out my original salutation, I replaced it with *Dear Friends,* then stared at the blank page for what felt like an hour before locking onto my first line: *Billy Chin is dead, and the Academy wants your money.* Thinking this witty, I emailed the sentence to Neil, who wrote back immediately, saying that I forgot to mention the new cafeteria and the boathouse we were planning to build.

Suddenly it was *we,* I noted. As if Neil and I were in on the planning, as if the cafeteria were ours, as if we'd be invited to the ceremony when Phil Ennis and company broke ground on the new boathouse. But that was the thing about Ennis. He had a real talent for roping people in and making them do his dirty work in a way that made them feel special, as if they were contributing to the greater glory of God by pestering fellow graduates with dinnertime phone calls, or calling in favors with local politicos to bend zoning laws so the Academy could continue its spiraling blitzkrieg through the crumbling neighborhoods of North Philadelphia.

The messages bounced back and forth between the two of us for the next hour, and the invitation evolved with a curious mix of loathing and affection for the institution that had, for better or for worse, brought us all together and turned us into the men we had become. One version had Ennis promising to loan me and Neil out as housemaids to whoever made the biggest donation in Billy's name—he'd provide the cleaning supplies if they provided the uniforms. Another version had him threatening to send Greg Packer to move in with anyone who didn't come out to mourn Billy's passing or at least send a few dead presidents to stand in their place.

Sure, Neil had made me promise not to fuck around, but this wasn't fucking around, exactly. At least, it wasn't public fucking around. It was private—a bit of banter between the two of us as we warmed up to write the real thing. Tastefully vague about the cause of Billy's death and the Academy's desire to profit from it, the clean version of the invitation we produced probably wasn't much different from anything that Frank Dearborn could have come up with; but the fact that it was ours, that Neil and I had written it together, sent a clear message to Ennis that we weren't just a couple of names at the bottom of a letter.

It said that Billy was our friend.

It said that we could speak for ourselves.

It said that Neil and I were adults, and we could each stand on our own two feet.

Or at least it would have, if I had forwarded the right version to Ennis. Five minutes after I sent the final draft, Neil responded to the copy he received with a single sentence: *I'd buy you a parachute if I knew it wouldn't open.*

Animal Crackers? I wrote back.

When the telephone rang, I knew I was in trouble. I'd made a mess of things before, but it was usually on a scale that Neil could contain. Like the time we drove sixty miles to see Elvis Costello in Atlantic City and I waited until he parked the car to mention that I'd left the tickets back in Philly. Or the time I picked a fight with a hairy Vietnam vet in a wheelchair and Neil said that I was off my medication to stop the guy from kicking my ass. Or the time I tried to pay a stripper by sliding a credit card between her breasts, and Neil kept her from having the bouncer beat the hell out of us by giving her all the cash left in his wallet. The fact that all three of these incidents occurred on the same night said a lot about how much slack Neil was willing to cut me. But the more I thought about it, the more I was beginning to realize that I was a bit of an asshole. Because it wasn't just that night, and it wasn't just the tickets, and it wasn't just the Vietnam vet and the stripper and the money Neil fronted to keep me out of trouble. It was all those things multiplied by all the days and all the nights and all the opportunities I took to throw a monkey wrench into the finely tuned mess that was my life.

"This is a joke, right?" Neil said. "Tell me you didn't just send that letter to Ennis."

I checked my outgoing email and clicked on the message in question. I didn't need to open the attached document to know what I had done, but I clicked on it anyway. What I thought had been a scream a few minutes earlier was suddenly turning my stomach with dread. In the final version of the letter—the wrong letter—Neil and I were finally coming out of the closet as the pair of gay lovers the football team had always pegged us for, and we were claiming Frank Dearborn as our love child. Billy Chin was watching over us from heaven, and every reference to Phil Ennis read, predictably, Fill Anus.

"Oh," I said. "I think I might have made a mistake."

"Jesus, Charley. *You're* the one who wanted Ennis to take us seriously for a change."

"Don't worry," I said. "I'll take care of it."

"How?" Neil asked.

"I'll call him," I said. "And tell him not to read it."

"And when he asks why?"

"It's an early draft," I said. "Full of typos."

"And if he's already seen it?"

"I'll say it was all me—that you had nothing to do with it."

"That isn't the point," Neil said. "You said it yourself. Ennis looks at guys like us and sees a bunch of zeroes. Once a year, we send him a check, and once a year we get a blurb in the alumni magazine about our shitty little jobs and how we'll never make anything of ourselves. This was our chance to actually do something—to show Ennis we could take something seriously for a change—and you went straight for the cheap laughs."

"It was an accident," I said. "I meant to send the other one."

"I almost believe you," Neil said.

"It's the truth," I said. "Why would I send the wrong letter on purpose?"

"I don't know," Neil said. "You have a tendency to do things that don't make any sense sometimes."

"Like what?" I said.

"Were you on the bridge with us yesterday?"

"Oh," I said. "That."

"And this ludicrous job of yours. What's that all about?"

"Okay," I said. "You're right. I've gotten myself into some weird shit lately. But don't worry. I'll take care of it."

"Whatever you're planning, count me out," Neil said. "Don't even mention my name."

"Neil," I said, but he'd already hung up.

❧ CHAPTER ELEVEN ❧

I sat at my desk with my head in my hands, the incriminating invitation to Billy Chin's memorial service glowing on the computer screen in front of me. Neil was right, I thought. I couldn't do anything without screwing it up. My job was a joke, my house was a mess, and the dissertation I'd begun the previous September was languishing in some dark, lifeless corner of my hard drive, as scraps of paper bearing the late night scrawl of half-hearted inspiration curled in on themselves, yellowing and dusty, among the long-overdue library books stacked at my elbows. On top of it all, there was Billy. Even his death couldn't keep me from failing him on a regular basis.

"Are you okay?" Karen asked, poking her head into the spare bedroom we used as an office. "You look like you're about to be sick."

"I think I screwed up," I said.

"What now?"

"Everything," I said. "My whole life."

"Is there any chance that you're exaggerating?"

"No," I said. "Everything I've ever done is a joke."

"As the woman you married, you can see why I might take offense at that."

"You know what I mean," I said. "I never take anything seriously."

"That's not true," Karen said. "What about Billy's memorial service?"

I shook my head.

"Fucked it up," I said. "The same way I fuck everything up. I turned it into a joke."

I looked up at Karen. She was dirty and sweaty from scrubbing the fine, filmy layer of wallpaper paste from our dining room walls. In less than a week, her students would take their final exams, and she'd be up to her ankles in red ink and bluebooks. Sure, she'd complain about it. And, sure, she was frustrated that our renovations weren't exactly going as well as she'd expected. But at least she was doing something—something positive, something constructive, something meaningful. Meanwhile, my biggest effort to date had been to avoid putting any effort into anything at all, and the consequences were starting to show.

"I need to act like an adult for a change," I said. "I need to do something with my life."

"Okay," Karen said. "Let's start with the dining room."

"No," I said. "I need to do something big."

"There's always the living room," she said. "And the upstairs hallway."

"Still too small," I said. "I want to do something important. Something major. Something epic. Something big enough to make up for this slump I'm in."

"You could always finish your dissertation," Karen said.

"It's a thought," I said.

"But I still think you should start with the dining room."

"You're hinting at something," I said.

"The boy catches on fast."

"I haven't been very helpful around here, have I?"

"Not exactly," Karen said. "No. In fact, *helpful* doesn't even begin to cover it. Even when you're here, you're not exactly here, if you know what I mean."

"Sorry," I said.

"I know you've had a rough couple of weeks, Charley, but—"

Before Karen could finish her thought, the telephone rang, and Greg Packer informed me that he had, in his words, the most auspicious of news. Evangeline, the woman he'd met online, had agreed to meet him for drinks. The only catch was that she still lived in Chicago and that Greg, caught up in the moment, had promised to meet her later that night.

"So what are you going to do?" I asked, mouthing to Karen that it was Greg on the phone.

"What else *can* I do? I've booked a flight to Chicago."

"That's ridiculous," I said as Karen rolled her eyes and left me alone to deal with my gentleman caller. "Where'd you get the money for that?"

"Mother has a vested interest in my love life."

"That's disturbing," I said.

"More specifically, she wants grandchildren."

"So she's sending you to Chicago to meet a strange woman for drinks," I said. "Makes perfect sense when you think about it."

"Your sarcasm notwithstanding, I've called to ask a favor. To wit, can you give me a ride to the airport?"

"What about your mother?" I said. "Can't she give you a ride?"

"We had a bit of a falling out after she bought the plane ticket," Greg said. "Mother wants us to raise the children here in Philadelphia, but I told her that Evangeline might well have a life and career in Chicago to consider."

"That was very big of you," I said.

"Indeed. And before you ask, I made the same request of our mutual friend regarding a ride to the airport, but he was in a particularly foul mood when I called."

"Neil?" I said.

"Yes," Greg said. "I won't repeat what he said to me, but it wasn't pretty."

This was perfect, I thought. If I got Greg out of his hair even for a day, Neil would have to forgive me. Or at least he'd have to admit that I wasn't a *complete* screw-up. An incomplete screw-up, perhaps, but giving Greg a ride to the airport was an important first step in digging myself out of the hole I was in.

"Okay," I said. "I'll give you a ride."

"Capital," Greg said. "Of course, we'll need to make a few stops along the way."

"Stops?" I said.

"For odds and ends. And, needless to say, I'll need to swing by the hospital for an epidural."

"I know your mom wants grandkids," I said. "But isn't that a little premature—not to mention the fact that you're a guy?"

"Your attempt at humor is duly noted, but I must point out, if only for your own edification, the subtle distinction between the anesthetic and steroid varieties of epidural. One, as you have accurately guessed, is closely associated with women in labor, but the other has myriad applications beyond the delivery room. For example, in my current condition, the prospect of sitting on an airplane for several hours is completely unfathomable without the aid of modern science. While pain medication is certainly an option, the enormity of the undertaking demands that I feel nothing from the neck down. That's a slight overstatement, of course, but for the purposes of alleviating the kind of agony I will undoubtedly confront as I embark upon my quest, nothing compares to an epidural."

"I stand corrected," I said.

"The flight leaves at three and I've scheduled the procedure for noon, so you can understand my desire for you to attend to my needs posthaste."

"Right," I said. "Posthaste."

The hard part was explaining the situation to Karen. Though I hadn't exactly promised to help her, she was well on her way to winning me over when Greg called. A few more seconds, and I would have been hers.

"What about our walls?" my wife asked as I stood in front of her, car keys in hand, my bungled attempt at explaining Greg's need for an epidural still lingering between us. "What about doing something with your life?"

"Don't you see?" I said. "This is even better."

"How is unleashing Greg Packer on some unsuspecting girl in Chicago better than helping me with the house?"

"Neil's been dealing with Greg's shit forever," I said. "If I step up and take Greg off his hands, that's one less thing for him to worry about. From there, who knows? I'll come home, I'll help with the walls, and then I'll iron things out with Ennis."

"What happened with Ennis?"

"Don't worry about Ennis," I said. "The point is, I'm taking control, and everything's going to work out fine."

❧ CHAPTER TWELVE ❧

Greg lived with his mother in a powder-blue mini-mansion on the wrong end of a partially gated community whose developers had made the profound miscalculation of building in the backyard of the area's busiest municipal airfield. For the most part, the only planes that came and went from the field were single-engine Cessnas, but the occasional corporate jet taxiing down the runway a mere three hundred yards from Greg's bedroom window had probably contributed to the delusion that meeting a woman for drinks in Chicago was a perfectly normal thing to do. At least that's what I told myself as I rang his doorbell a second time and waited for someone to answer. Otherwise, the only explanation was that Greg had completely lost touch with reality.

When someone finally answered the door, it was Greg's mother.

"Is this about the lawn?" she asked, peering at me from behind a brass door chain. "Because if it's about the lawn, we've already hired someone to take care of it."

Behind me, the overgrown lawn lapped at the sidewalk, and the shrubs in front of Greg's house grew wild and unkempt beneath dark, sealed windows.

"No," I shouted as what was either a tiny airplane or a very large mosquito buzzed angrily somewhere behind Greg's house. "I'm here for Greg. He called about a ride to the airport."

"You must be Karen's boyfriend," the woman said, undoing the chain and letting me into her dim, stuffy house. "Greg's told me so much about her."

"Husband," I said. "I'm Karen's husband."

"Husband, boyfriend." The woman was plump and pale with tiny eyes and bleached blonde hair. "It's not like the glue's settled yet. Am I right? Greg's in the Christmas room."

I'd heard rumors of the Christmas room, but I never believed in it until Greg's mother said the words aloud. According to Neil, it was Mrs. Packer's refuge, an alternate dimension where it was always the most wonderful time of the year. It also doubled as what Greg referred to as his war room, and when his mother opened the door, he looked up from his computer with a scowl and instructed her to show me in.

"He's a little anxious," Greg's mother whispered aloud as she left me alone with her son. "First date and all."

"Mother, please!" Greg sighed.

So this was what Neil had to deal with on a fairly regular basis, I thought as Nat King Cole sang of chestnuts roasting on an open fire and Jack Frost nipping at my nose. No wonder he wanted to move to Maryland.

Meticulously decorated with crystal ornaments and shimmering tinsel, a Christmas tree stood guard over a king's ransom in empty gift-wrapped packages. Next to the tree stood a three-quarter-scale manger scene complete with donkeys, shepherds, and wise men all carved out of pine. An electric train ran circles around the feet of the magi, and when I looked up, I saw that the ceiling was painted with a heavenly host of angels.

"So," I said. "Which are the cherubim and which are the seraphim?"

"Before you jump to any conclusions, I should point out that those aren't paintings. They're merely decals that mother purchased at a crafts fair. The woman isn't completely insane."

"Of course not," I said, eyeing a bookshelf lined with Santa Claus figurines. "Are you ready to go?"

"My bags are upstairs, if you'd be so kind."

"Bags?" I said. "You're meeting this woman for drinks."

"But there's no telling where the evening will take us. I'm sure you'll agree that a man needs to be prepared."

"Prepared, sure. But it's not like you're moving in with the girl."

"One never knows," Greg said.

Arguing with the guy was like drowning in quicksand, so I gave up on talking any sense into him and went upstairs to grab his suitcases.

Standing impatiently at the door in his rumpled blue blazer, Greg checked his watch as I struggled with the bags and his mother pinned a lime-green carnation to his lapel.

"Isn't my son handsome?" Mrs. Packer asked, beaming with pride as Gene Autry sang "Frosty the Snowman" in the adjoining room.

"Sure thing," I said, setting the bags down to catch my breath at the bottom of the stairs. "A real lady killer."

"I'm sorry, Mother, but we're in a bit of a hurry," Greg said, gesturing for me to keep moving. "So if you don't mind, I'll take my leave."

"Of course, darling," Greg's mother said, following us only as far as the front door, as if stepping into the daylight might reduce her to a pile of ash. "Don't forget to smile. And remember to mention that you're a lawyer. Women love lawyers."

"You're a lawyer?" I said, hefting Greg's luggage into my Saturn.

"Technically, yes," Greg said. "But only in New Jersey."

WE WERE barely out of Greg's cul-de-sac when he started adjusting my passenger seat and complaining about its lack of lumbar support. A sure sign of a quality automobile, he explained, punching the buttons on my radio and cranking up the air conditioner, was lumbar support. Neil's car had good lumbar support, he said. And a better sound system, and a much more effective air conditioner.

"Well, we're not in Neil's car, are we?" I said.

"Clearly not," Greg agreed. "Do you mind if I ask you a personal question?"

"That depends," I said. "How personal?"

"Does Karen ever ask about me?"

"Not really," I said.

"Then what does she say when my name comes up in conversation?"

"It doesn't," I said.

"That's very surprising," Greg said. "I thought we had a connection. Your wife and I. Something profound and spiritual—as if we're cut from the same cloth."

"That's a very disturbing thought, Greg."

"She and I should spend more time together," Greg said, ignoring my comment. "Especially now that Neil's moving. As you know, I've come to rely very heavily upon him for advice, conversation, moral support, and other services too numerous to mention, both tangible and intangible. While these are certainly appropriate demands to place upon a friend of his caliber, Neil's pending move has forced me to reevaluate where he stands in my life. To put it as bluntly as possible, I need a new best friend, and I'm hoping that Karen might be interested in the job."

"I'll mention it to her," I said. "But you might want to keep your options open."

"While your advice on the topic is certainly appreciated, I believe the matter is best left up to the principals in question, namely myself and Karen."

"Absolutely," I said, and Greg suggested we stop at a gas station to stock up on provisions.

Watching me wander through a maze of snack chips, dog treats, air fresheners, and cans of motor oil in the all-seeing curvature of a security mirror, Greg leaned against a shaky Coca-Cola display and told me what to pick up. Breath mints for close conversation, he shouted—and perhaps deep kissing if it should come to that. Beef jerky for stamina. *People* magazine for small talk, and *Maxim* for all the latest sexual techniques.

"I'm a little rusty when it comes to activity between the sheets," he confessed to me, the cashier, and an elderly woman whose only crime was stopping at the local gas-n-go for a gallon of milk on a Saturday morning. "In fact, I'd be much obliged if you could offer me a few pointers before my flight leaves."

Making a show of poring over the magazine rack, I looked up at the security mirror and shrugged my shoulders. There was no *Maxim*, I shouted, hoping the cashier wouldn't call my bluff. The last thing I wanted was for Greg to attempt any of the TEN SECRETS FOR DRIVING HER WILD advertised on the cover. When he suggested that *Cosmo* would do just as well so long as he remembered to follow all of the instructions in reverse, I shrugged my shoulders again and said there were no sex magazines at all. The best I could offer him was a copy of *Guns and Ammo*, which, after giving the matter due consideration, he decided was better than nothing.

"I want you to know something," Greg said as he handed the cashier his mother's credit card. "If anything should ever happen to you, I swear on my mother's life that I'll spend the rest of eternity watching over Karen."

"You're not planning to kill me, are you, Greg?"

I was only half-joking, but I told the cashier not to bother with a bag on the off chance that Greg might try to suffocate me with it the next time I turned my head to check for oncoming traffic.

"Of course I'm not planning to kill you," Greg said. "As you know, I'm fiercely loyal. All I'm saying is that accidents can happen. Look at Billy Chin, for example."

"That wasn't an accident," I said. "Billy killed himself."

"The evidence would suggest otherwise."

"What evidence?" I asked. "What are you talking about?"

"That he went to the Academy, of course. Donkeys don't do that kind of thing."

"That's the dumbest thing I've ever heard."

"My solemn belief is that Billy's death was an accident," Greg said as we walked back to my car. "The alternative is too mind-boggling to comprehend. I have constructed for myself a perfectly balanced model of the universe based upon principles you and I both learned at the feet of our mentors when we walked the hallowed halls of our alma mater. To date, this model has never failed me. Indeed, it has guided me through college, law school, and numerous confrontations with my mother. I have utilized this model of the universe to analyze and understand the behavior of my fellow man, the ebb and flow of geopolitical power relations the world over, the statistical likelihood of the existence of God, the outcomes of three Super Bowls, and what I consider the final frontier of all human knowledge: the fleeting, hidden and often contradictory desires which motivate that most mysterious and fickle of species. I am referring, of course, to woman. If Billy Chin killed himself, then all of my other conclusions must be called into question. I'm sure you understand that on the eve of my latest campaign, such a proposition cannot even be considered.

Now, about those pointers we were discussing. Is Karen into anything kinky?"

⚓

THE HOSPITAL smelled of ammonia and body odor, and I couldn't decide whether that was better or worse than the musky aroma that had gradually overtaken my car since Greg settled into the passenger seat earlier that morning. The issue, however, was rendered moot when a tall, skinny man in a turquoise windbreaker skidded to a halt in front of the admitting desk and said that his wife was in labor. She was in the parking lot, he said, and she needed a wheelchair.

"Better make that two," I said, sidling up next to him.

"First time?" the man asked.

"Yeah," I said.

"Nervous?" he asked.

"Not especially," I said. "To tell you the truth, I'm not really invested in any of this."

Two orderlies arrived, and we led them to our respective cars. As luck would have it, the man in the windbreaker had parked right next to my Saturn, and Greg was offering the mother-to-be advice on nutrition, early education, and disease prevention.

"There are a million things that can go wrong before the child is even born," Greg said as he sank into his wheelchair. "The mere fact that you've brought this baby to term is, needless to say, a minor miracle in and of itself, but now you have to worry about such childhood diseases as mumps, measles, chickenpox, polio, and rubella, as well as the adverse effects of the so-called inoculations against the same. Though I don't have the exact numbers, I understand that while infant mortality rates have declined significantly in modern times, there remains the statistical reality that the first three years of life are the most hazardous to any child."

"Jesus," the man in the windbreaker said as the orderlies pushed Greg and the pregnant woman toward the hospital at an even pace. "Sweet, sweet Jesus."

"Then, of course, you have to consider any number of threats originating outside the home as well. Kidnapping, for example. Murder. Drugs. Indeed, any number of crimes too heinous to mention in mixed company."

A pair of glass doors slid open in front of us, and the pregnant couple took the lead.

"A bit of advice," Greg called out as they disappeared around a corner. "Demand the epidural. It's the only way to fly."

Greg's orderly wheeled him into an elevator, and the door slid shut behind them. Over the next hour, pregnant women continued to roll into the hospital with men in various stages of panic trailing close behind. Taking a seat in a row of plastic bleachers, I overheard a man with silver hair and a hot appendix dictating his last will and testament to a teenage girl in candy stripes and braces. On the television overhead, the members of a high school basketball team were trying to convince their star forward to give up smoking.

Dropping some coins into a snack machine, I bought a bag of miniature hard pretzels and thought about slipping quickly and quietly out of the hospital. Not only for myself, of course, but for the woman who was waiting for Greg in Chicago. If anything happened to her, I'd have to live with the guilt for the rest of my life. And if by some obscene miracle she and Greg got together, then the world would have me to blame for whatever fate befell humanity as a result of their unholy union. Besides, I couldn't shake the thought, irrational as it was, that Greg might really be planning to kill me in a misguided bid to win Karen's affection. By the time I decided to run, however, it was too late. The procedure was finished, and Greg was rolling toward me with a wide grin plastered across his face.

"The omens are clear, my friend," he said as a new orderly wheeled him out to the parking lot. "The procedure was a success, and I'm a new man. Clearly the gods have smiled upon us. Now onward to the airport, then forward to Chicago for victory."

Accounting for traffic, I guessed I had about forty-five minutes to convince Greg that the trip was a bad idea. Greg, however, had only one thing on his mind, and as soon as he was buckled into his seat, he started badgering me about the mechanics of what he insisted on referring to as sexual congress. Was it true, he wanted to know, that the likelihood of bringing a woman to orgasm could be increased via the strategic placement of pillows?

"I realize that discussing the issue in relation to Karen is off the table," he added. "So feel free to speak in the most general of terms. In your opinion, what's the most efficient way to pleasure a woman?"

"I'm not sure you should be so worried about efficiency," I said. "Let's focus on staying out of jail."

"Jail?" Greg said. "Don't be ridiculous."

"If she calls it a night, let her go. If she says she's having fun, don't assume it means anything. Even if she invites you back to her place—"

"No means no. I understand completely."

"Do you?" I asked.

"Yes, and while I appreciate your concern for my well-being, I must point out that I do have a law degree and am therefore particularly attuned to the legalities of courtship. In addition to stocking up on breath mints and beef jerky, I've taken the liberty of drawing up a contract outlining our pre- and post-coital duties to each other. While this contract exists primarily to protect myself and the rights of any offspring our lovemaking might generate, it serves as a *de facto* guarantee of her rights as well. To put it bluntly, she doesn't get any of *this* until she signs on the dotted line."

Greg pointed at his crotch, and we drove the rest of the way in silence.

WHEN I dumped Greg off at the airport, he pressed a wrinkled dollar bill into the palm of my hand and said that although future generations might never know the part I played in keeping the Packer line alive, he, for one, would never forget. Disturbing as this thought may have been, I pocketed his dollar, and started to make a mental list of all the things that separated me from Greg. Number one was the fact that I was married. Number two was my gainful employment, but then I remembered what I did for a living and that in my whole history of working I'd never done anything especially gainful. This left me with the fact that I didn't live with my mother, but the loophole there was that in Greg's twisted view of the world, a mother and a wife served roughly the same purpose. Though I preferred to assume that the purpose he had in mind had more to do with housekeeping than his quest for an heir, it was impossible to deny the Bates Motel vibe emanating from their home—unless, of course, you were either Greg or his mother, in which case, everything seemed perfectly normal. Which, oddly enough, I saw as my salvation. While Greg had no idea that his life was so screwed up, I was acutely and obsessively aware of what a mess I tended to make of things on a fairly regular basis. Whether or not this heightened level of awareness made me any better or worse than Greg was beside the point. What mattered most, I told myself again and again, was that I was different.

When I got home, Karen asked how my date with Greg had gone. She'd finished scrubbing three of the four dining room walls, and though the filmy layer of sweat and grime that covered her skin had grown thicker in my absence, her question made me feel as if I were the one who needed a long, hot shower.

"Don't ask," I said.

"It was that bad?"

"He wants to be your best friend."

"Don't even joke about it."

"I'm serious," I said. "But don't worry. If things work out with this woman in Chicago, I'm sure he'll forget all about you."

"That's comforting," Karen said.

"You don't think I'm like him, do you?" I asked.

"You? Like Greg Packer?" She wrinkled her nose and put her arms around my waist. "I don't think so, Charley."

"What I mean is, do you think Neil gets home and has this same conversation with Madeline about how crazy I am? About how I'm a huge pain in the ass?"

"Are you kidding? He'd do anything for you."

"Just like he'd do anything for Greg."

"That's different. You're his best friend."

"Yeah, but for how long?" I asked.

And how far can I push him before he'll give up on me?

"I wouldn't worry about it," Karen said. "You're nothing like Greg Packer."

"I hope not," I said.

"Trust me," Karen said. "You're not."

All I wanted was to believe her, so I dipped a scrub brush into the warm, gray water of her bucket and went to work on the fourth wall of our dining room.

CHAPTER THIRTEEN

Despite my best intentions, Monday morning found me lying flat on my back again, balloons tied to my wrist, water dripping into my unwieldy costume as the sprinklers came to life on the lawn in front of the bank. Little by little, I was getting used to the idea that Neil was leaving. Maryland wasn't *too* far away, I told myself—certainly not far enough to keep Greg Packer from showing up on Neil's doorstep if, perchance, he stumbled upon a woman in the DC area who was willing to meet him for drinks. But it was enough distance to ensure that Neil wouldn't be around to get the rest of us out of whatever jams we managed to get ourselves into.

He wouldn't be around to broker deals between Greg and his mother when their squabbles drove Greg out of the house and onto the sofa of some poor, unfortunate friend. He wouldn't be around to coordinate lunches and dinners with Sean Sullivan, Dwayne Coleman, Anthony Gambacorta, and anyone else who bothered to keep in touch with us after we graduated from the Academy. And he definitely wasn't going to be around to get me back on my feet whenever I slipped in the mud—literally or otherwise.

What all of this meant in practical terms was that our little gang of misfits was going to need a new leader, and as I lay on my back in the stuffy, damp darkness of my giant dollar sign, I could think of no better candidate than myself.

In Neil's absence, I would be the new Neil.

My first course of action in this regard was to call Phil Ennis and clear up any bad blood that might have resulted from the letter I'd forwarded to him over the weekend. It was all my doing, I'd tell him, and Neil had nothing to do with it. It was embarrassing and terrible and something I'd always regret. If I could take it back, I'd do it in a heartbeat. The letter, I imagined myself insisting as I found Ennis's number on the speed dial of my cell phone, did not reflect my true feelings for the Academy, which were nothing but positive. From here on out, I'd be a team player. Whatever Ennis needed, I'd provide without a second's hesitation.

"Do you know what your problem is, Schwartz?" Ennis said before I could hurl myself onto my sword.

"No," I said, forcing a chipper tone. "But I'm willing to learn."

"*That*," Ennis said. "That right there is your problem."

"That I'm willing to learn?" I said.

"No, Schwartz," Ennis said. "Your attitude. You think your hands are clean just because you're a cynic. Well, let me tell you something—the rest of us have to live in the real world. The rest of us have bills to pay. The rest of us need to get our hands dirty so we can get shit done, so fuck you, Schwartz, if you can't deal with it. Fuck you, fuck your idealism, and fuck your naive grasp of how the fucking world works. Do you know how much money it costs to run this place? Do you know how many kids are here on bullshit grants and scholarships? Do you know how many parents never pay their tuition on time? Do you think I like wearing a shit-eating grin every time I meet an asshole with deep pockets? Do you think I like hitting alums up for cash every goddamn day? I don't, Schwartz, but it's my job, and if you don't like it, you can go to hell."

"Look, I'm calling to apologize, okay?"

Ennis said nothing, but I could imagine him sitting at his desk and trying to regain his composure. At the end of the day, I represented money—maybe only a small amount, but money nonetheless. And if he could still use my name to squeeze a few more dollars out of my graduating class, then so much the better.

"Okay, Schwartz," he eventually said in a strangled tone that suggested he was doing his utmost to rein in his palpable rage. "Let me tell you how this is going to work. When I get off the phone with you, I'm reaching out to your graduating class, I'm reaching out to some key alums, I'm reaching out to the community, and I'm reaching out to the media. From this point on, it's a full-court press. Do you understand?"

"I understand," I said. "But why the media?"

"You're obviously not a newspaper man," Ennis said with undisguised contempt. "We've been taking hits in the *Inquirer* ever since we put in the new parking lot. They say we destroyed the neighborhood when all we ever did was tear down a few abandoned houses. But if we invite a few local kids into the school and talk about how we're taking donations in Billy's name to help fund our new initiative to get Philly boys in the door, it might help win a few hearts and minds, if you'll pardon the expression."

"So, what? This is all a big PR campaign for the Raging Donkeys?"

"Enough with the moralizing, Schwartz. Are you in or out?"

"I'm in," I said, reminding myself that I was trying to be the new Neil. "I'm in. Definitely."

"Good," Ennis said. "We've been presented with an opportunity to take something positive away from what, by all counts, is a tragic situation. Your job in all of this is to answer any and all questions about Billy with the simple facts that he was a kindhearted soul and that he loved the Academy. And at the end of all this, when we all sit down to remember Billy, you'll get up and say a few pleasant words, and we'll all feel good for having known him. Can you handle that?"

"Absolutely," I said. "No problem."

"And from now on, you report to Frank Dearborn."

"Oh," I said. "*That* might be a problem."

"I don't want to hear it, Schwartz. Whatever you have against Frank, get over it. Otherwise—"

"No," I said. "You're right. I'll get over it. We'll have dinner together. Catch up on old times. It'll be a riot."

"Watch the sarcasm, Schwartz," Ennis said. "You're hanging by a thread as it is."

I took a breath to apologize, but Ennis had already hung up on me. Though my first instinct was to call the bastard back and tell him that we must have been cut off, I let out my breath and reminded myself that if I wanted to be the new Neil, I had to do the kind of things Neil did—which, above all, meant avoiding the kind of things *I* usually did, like flying off the handle every time someone pissed me off.

TRUE TO his word, Ennis didn't waste any time sending an email about the memorial service to everyone he knew. I know this because I'd barely gotten off the line with him when my cell phone started to ring—and ring, and ring, and ring. Which meant that I spent the next hour-and-a-half listening to a gospel choir tell me that I was moving on up to a deluxe apartment on the East Side, while fielding phone calls from people I hadn't spoken to in years. They all wanted to know what happened to Billy, and when I told them that his death had been a suicide, there was always an awkward pause. As Greg Packer's unbending model of the universe insisted, the information just didn't compute, so I filled the silence with only the details that cushioned the blow.

He was in a bad place, I said, echoing the words Neil had used when I first broke the news to him. He always loved the Academy, I said, repeating only some of the information that Billy's mother had given me. I left out any mention of the Henry Avenue Bridge. I left out the fact that he had jumped to his death. I left out the line of stitches I'd seen running up his arm on New Year's Eve. Instead, I talked about the memorial service and how I hoped to see everyone there. To honor Billy's memory, I added. And his love for the Academy.

After fielding a dozen or so calls, I was about to turn off my phone when Greg Packer called to give me the rundown on his expedition to the windy city.

"The mission was a failure," he said before I could say hello. "Evangeline used the F-word."

"The F-word?" I said.

In the distance, I could hear footsteps squishing across the lawn.

"*Friend*," Greg said. "Can you believe that? She wants to be friends. I tried to persuade her otherwise, but she wouldn't have it."

"I'd love to chat, Greg," I said as the footsteps drew closer. "But now isn't the time."

Was this it, I wondered? My performance review?

"Nonsense," Greg said. "No time like the present."

Craning my neck, I pressed an eye to one of the vents in the shoulder of my costume, but all I could see was a pair of black leather boots.

"Sorry, Greg," I said. "But I have to go."

Greg tried to protest, but I turned off my phone just in time to hear someone speak my name. It was a voice I knew, but one I hadn't heard in a while. A man's voice—and more important, unless she'd started smoking much more heavily than usual, not Sue's.

"Is that you, Schwartz?"

"Anthony?" I said, shouting at his feet from inside my dollar sign. "Gambacorta?"

"Neil said I could find you here."

"Remind me to thank him," I said. "How was the *Dukes of Hazzard* marathon?"

If Anthony had any inkling that I was taking a shot at him for missing dinner with me and Neil the first time we tried to raise money in Billy's name, he didn't let on. Instead, he told me that he'd recorded the marathon in question and was editing together a compilation of Daisy Duke's best scenes. He'd sell me a copy if I wanted one, he added, but that wasn't the main reason he wanted to talk to me.

"I had an idea, Schwartz. About the Billy Chin Festival."

"It's not exactly a festival," I said. "It's more of a memorial service."

"Exactly," Anthony said. "And what better way to remember Billy than with the magic of theater?"

"What do you have in mind?" I said. "A revival of *Fellatio!*"

"Better," Anthony said. "The world premiere of *Down in the Stalag.*"

"The *Hogan's Heroes* musical?" I said, reminding myself once again to be diplomatic if only because that was how Neil would handle the situation. "I'm not sure Billy's memorial service is the right venue for that. Besides, it's only three weeks away, and that doesn't give you much time to put everything together."

"Not a problem. I threw *Hung Jury* together in half that time."

"*Hung Jury*?" I said, regretting the words as soon as I'd spoken them.

"A nude version of *Twelve Angry Men*. You didn't hear about it?"

"I guess I missed it."

"Anyway, I was thinking we could do it in the Academy's new theater and dedicate the show to Billy. You're still in touch with Greg Packer, right?"

"Unfortunately," I said. "What does he have to do with anything?"

"Are you kidding? He'd make the perfect Sergeant Schlitz."

"I thought it was Schultz," I said.

"On TV, yeah. But I had to make a few adjustments for legal purposes. Hogan is Logan—I'll be playing *him*, of course. Klink is Klein. Schultz is Schlitz. Do you want to see the script? You'd make a great Newhouse."

"I don't think so," I said.

"You're saying no?"

"I'm saying I don't want anything to do with it."

"You don't understand," Anthony said, going down on one knee and speaking directly into the narrow slot that afforded my main view of the outside world. "This could be big. If the right people see it, I can really go places."

"What people?" I said.

"The media," Anthony said. "Didn't you get the email? Ennis sent it to *everybody*. All I'm asking is that you read the script. You at least owe me that much."

More than likely, Anthony was correct about what I owed him, but only due to a technicality. Towards the end of our senior year at the Academy, Anthony and I had agreed to be roommates when we both found out that we'd be attending the same college come autumn. As things turned out, this was a bad idea—a fact I should have recognized when, independent of each other, Neil, Dwayne, and Sean all asked if I'd lost my mind after I told them that Anthony and I would be rooming together. It wasn't so much that Anthony was a terrible person, they all agreed, as the fact that living with him would pose certain logistical problems involving the maintenance and storage of his wardrobe and vast collection of hair-care products, not to mention pornography. At the same time, my lack of respect for other people's property wasn't going to help matters a whole lot either, so no one was the least surprised when the whole relationship went up in flames the night I invited the men's rugby team into our room to try on all of Anthony's clothes and rummage through his porn. So, yes, maybe I did have a moral obligation to read *Down in the Stalag*, but I just couldn't bring myself to do it—even if I *was* trying to be the new Neil.

"I don't think it'll make much of a difference," I said. "But if you really want to do this, the guy you want to talk to is Ennis."

"I didn't know he was into theater," Anthony said.

"He's not," I said. "He's into money. How much are you willing to part with?"

"So, what?" Anthony said. "This is all about cash?"

"That's about the long and short of it."

"Can I mention your name? Tell Ennis you're on board?"

"Do whatever you want," I said.

"Sweet," Anthony said, already squishing his way back to the parking lot. "I won't forget this, Charley. I promise. When *Down in the Stalag* hits Broadway, you're getting an Executive Producer credit."

He was halfway across the lawn when I switched on my phone and remembered why, despite my shenanigans with the rugby team, I didn't owe him a thing.

"Wait!" I screamed as the gospel choir resumed its maddening serenade. "Anthony! You need to fix my cell phone!"

"No time!" Anthony shouted back. "I have a musical to produce!"

"Bastard," I muttered as I scrolled through my messages.

In the time it took Anthony to pitch *Down in the Stalag*, my cell phone had logged seventeen missed calls and taken four messages—three from Greg Packer and one from Frank Dearborn.

Apparently we'd been cut off, Greg said, his low, guttural voice slurping in my ear as he delivered the very line

I'd been tempted to foist upon Ennis when he hung up on me earlier that morning. Perhaps, he added, I should think about selecting a new provider for my wireless service. One that wouldn't drop so many calls. One that respected the meaning of friendship. One that recognized the duty of every Raging Donkey to comfort his fellow man, particularly in times of heartbreak and pain. Needless to say, he concluded, such wireless providers were increasingly difficult to come by lately, and though he had no expectation of finding one for himself anytime in the near future, he hoped that I might have better luck than he would.

In case I missed it, Greg explained in his next message, he wasn't really talking about cell phone providers at all. He was talking about friends, and he couldn't believe I'd hung up on him. In his time of need, no less. In his darkest hour. What kind of friend was I, he demanded? Was this how I treated everyone?

I thought about Billy as Greg's second message bled into his third. How many calls had I failed to return? How many emails? How many times had my mind drifted when he was talking about—

God, I couldn't even remember anything we'd ever talked about.

In his own self-absorbed way, Greg was right.

What kind of friend was I?

The tail end of Greg's third message more or less told me to go to hell, and then Frank Dearborn was on the line asking if Karen and I were available for dinner on Friday. We could certainly do with some catching up, he said. And while we were at it, maybe we could work out some more of the details surrounding the Billy Chin Festival.

Festival, I thought? Why did that word keep popping up?

Whatever the reason, I could almost hear Ennis breathing down Frank's neck, pulling his strings, and forcing him to call me—or at least to call my bluff. If I were really serious about being a team player, I'd swallow my pride and sit down to dinner with the guy. Not that I had to like it, of course. Frank was still a pompous asshole and a racist to boot, not to mention the fact that his trust fund probably spouted more money in a week than I could make walking to the moon and back dressed as a giant dollar sign.

But I could do it, I told myself.

If only to prove that I was the better man.

❧ CHAPTER FOURTEEN ❧

The week dragged on, and the messages piled up—disembodied voices on my answering machine and cell phone, names and numbers scribbled on uneven scraps of paper. By Thursday, Karen had stopped bothering to answer the phone altogether. We were scrubbing the upstairs hallway by then, and Karen wanted to put a layer of paint on the walls before final exams forced her to take a break from what had evolved into an apparently endless undertaking.

"I forgot to tell you," I said as the telephone rang and Karen continued to scrub away at the plaster outside of our bedroom, "I told Frank Dearborn that we'd have dinner with him and his wife on Friday."

"That's tomorrow." Karen said. "How long have you known about this?"

"Not long," I said. "A day or so. But you have to understand—I've been busy with the Billy Chin Festival."

"Festival?" Karen asked

"Memorial service," I said, silently cursing the slip of my tongue. "Billy's memorial service is what I meant."

Since Monday, I'd heard the phrase *Billy Chin Festival* repeated so often that it was starting to take root in my mind—as if Billy were a sainted figure from years gone by, the martyred founder of some long-forgotten movement, the only reminder of which was the amorphous festival that still bore his name. Technically speaking, I was only supposed to be answering questions about Billy's death with the pleasantries that Ennis had prescribed, but when the calls turned to other matters—queries from businesses large and small about setting up tables and kiosks and handing out fliers to promote their goods and services, for example—I responded with the enthusiasm of the newly converted and agreed to every proposal that came my way. Because I was a go-getter now. Because I was a team player. Because I was the new Neil.

And so what if Ennis still had to approve everything I was agreeing to? He'd approve a Jim Jones Kool-Aid stand if a big enough donation was involved. The important thing— the thing I stressed to everyone who called—was that they mention my name when they spoke to him, that they specifically say that Charley Schwartz loved whatever the hell they were proposing. If Ennis heard my name enough times and in relation to enough dollar signs, he'd have to take me seriously. More to the point, he'd have to see that I could eat shit and come up smiling as professionally as anyone—including Frank Dearborn. If a festival was what he wanted, then that's what I'd deliver, no questions asked. All to honor Billy Chin, of course. All in the spirit of Saint Leonard de Noblac.

All in the name of our precious Academy.

"So what are we bringing?" Karen asked, dipping her scrub brush into her bucket and resuming her work without so much as a look in my direction.

"Bringing?" I said.

"To dinner," Karen said. "At Frank's house."

"Why would we bring anything?" I asked.

"Because that's what people do, Charley. When you visit someone's house, you bring something."

"But this is Frank Dearborn we're talking about. Antichrist at large. Racist extraordinaire. Unmitigated asshole. Did I tell you how he used to torture Billy?"

"You may have mentioned it," Karen said. "But that's not the point. The point is that we need to bring something, and you need to call him to find out what."

"Do I have to?" I said.

"What are you? Twelve? Pick up the phone and call."

"Can't I just email?"

"Would you just—" Karen said, exasperation choking off whatever she meant to say next. "Please? Charley?"

Karen glanced up from her endless scrubbing long enough to give me a look that said she wasn't kidding, so I grabbed my phone and went downstairs to check my latest slew of messages, pretending all along that I was on a call with Frank.

Charley, it's Greg, the first message began as I asked the empty dining room if I could speak to Frank. *I apologize profusely for any undue consternation my previous communiqués may have caused. I just got off the phone with Anthony Gambacorta, and I now realize that the only reason you ended our last discussion so abruptly and, I must add in all good conscience, rudely, is that you were in the middle of intense negotiations with Anthony regarding my role in his latest musical. He didn't state this fact explicitly, of course, but he did say that he met with you earlier this week, and the time frames certainly match up. As a result, I can only draw one conclusion: You were boldly and vigorously lobbying Anthony on my behalf. For this, I thank you and hasten to add that your name shall forever be on the lips of my sons and daughters and all generations of Packers to come. You will be remembered forever, Charley Schwartz, as my friend and ally, my constant companion, my footman, my attendant, my loyal—*

My voicemail cut him off, and I asked my phone if there was anything Karen and I could bring to Frank's house. By way of a response, a reporter from a Chinese-language newspaper asked if Billy had a birth name that might translate more freely to pictogram before leaving a number where I could get back to her. After that, a producer from a local cable news station offered to cover what was now almost solely referred to as the Billy Chin Festival, if we could manage to postpone the event until February when he could tie the story to a piece the station was planning for the Chinese New Year.

"A bottle of wine?" I nearly shouted. "You're sure that's all we can bring?"

Hey, the next message began. *It's Neil. Sorry for being a dick on Saturday. Give me a call sometime, okay? I got a weird message from Greg, and I'm not sure what to make of it. Something about fighting a restraining order in Chicago.*

"Red or white?" I said loud enough for Karen to hear me upstairs.

I couldn't really understand what he was saying because he was shouting in German. Do you know anything about this?

"Sounds good, Frank," I said in case Karen was still listening. "We're looking forward to it, too."

Anyway, I think he's losing it.

"See you then," I said.

Maybe we should do something. What do you think?

"Okay," I said in my friendliest voice.

Like I said, give me a call sometime.

"Right," I said. "Bye."

Bye, Neil said, and the messages rolled along.

Charley, this is Paul Tower. I graduated a few years before you did and just got the news about Billy Ching. Was it a rock-climbing accident? All I heard was something about the Henry Avenue Bridge, and I know a lot of climbers hang out around there. On the down-low, of course. A lot of midnight rappelling and that sort of thing. In any case, I opened a sporting goods store a few years back, and I was thinking we should get together and brainstorm some ways I might be able to help out with this festival thing you're having in his memory. Maybe a booth of some kind? I could probably throw together a quick demo of the latest equipment. *If you want, I can even set up a rock-climbing wall in the gym so everyone can see how fun and safe the sport can be as long as they have the right equipment. Sound good?*

Not especially, I thought, but I made a note to call him back anyway. A few hundred bucks for the booth. A couple of grand to set up a rock-climbing wall. It all added up in the Academy's favor, and the guy could always write off the expense as a gift to a tax-deductible charity organization.

Charley? It's Sue. We still need to schedule your performance review, but our mutual acquaintance told me to call about—what was it—the Billy Chun festival? He wants to know if you can distribute our usual PR stuff. Have you done that before? Or do you just work the lawn? I should know these things, shouldn't I? In any case, give me a call or talk to me the next time you're in. And don't forget that performance review. It's very important.

When Sue said "PR stuff," my guess was that she was talking about printing a stack of counterfeit hundred-dollar bills with Billy's face on the front and information on opening an account at any of the bank's fourteen convenient locations on the back. Not the most tasteful of ways to remember my friend, I thought, though I made a note to talk to her about it anyway—most likely during my performance review, and even then only to remind her that I was still working through the death of a close friend.

Hey, Charley, it's Sean Sullivan. Listen, I can get us a good deal on a moon bounce from Mr. Monkeybounce. They rent inflatable gorillas to us here at the car lot, and they're willing to let us have some kind of bouncy thing for next to nothing. Well, kind of. I mean, the guys at the lot said they'll pay for it as long as we can do some promotional stuff. Nothing big, of course. Just some fliers. A sign. Maybe a few business cards. Anyway, give me a call if you think that would work for the festival. And think some more about trading in your Saturn, okay?

Charley. Joe Viola. Veggies or doughnuts? I need to know.

Charley! It's Glenn Steiner. Long time, huh? Here's what I'm thinking for this Billy Chin thing. Silk screen banners, full-color, twenty-by-thirty on either side of the chapel. Billy's face, my logo, then something along the lines of Kibbleconnection.com is proud to join you in celebrating the life of our beloved friend Billy Chin. A real Chairman Mao look, if that helps you picture it. Give me a call and let me know what you think.

Hey, buddy, it's Frank. Maya says bring dessert. Can you swing that?

"Buddy?" I muttered. "Where the hell did you get that idea?"

We were acquaintances at best—two grown men with nothing in common beyond the high school we attended and the classmate we were both compelled to remember.

"So we're bringing wine?" Karen asked, lugging the bucket of dirty water down the stairs and across the floor on her way to the kitchen sink.

"No," I said. "Dessert."

"I thought you said wine."

"I did?" I asked, recalling my fake conversation with Frank a split-second too late. "I mean, I did, but then Frank called back and said to bring dessert instead."

"That's weird," Karen said. "I didn't hear the phone ring."

"I was on the other line," I said. "Checking my messages."

"Anything good?"

"Not really," I said. "What do you think you'll do for dessert?"

"Me?" Karen said. "Why am I making dessert?"

"You can't expect me to do it," I said. "I'm no good in the kitchen."

"And that's an excuse?"

"Not an excuse, exactly. An explanation. We each have our own talents. You're good at cooking, I'm good at—"

I stopped to think as Karen dumped her bucket of gray water into the kitchen sink.

"I'm waiting," Karen said. "What are you good at?"

"Give me a minute," I said. "I'm sure I can think of something."

"Don't worry about it, Charley. I'll take care of dessert."

"No," I said. "I mean, if it's a big deal."

"It's not a big deal. I just wish you'd pick up a little more of the slack around here."

"I know," I said. "I'm sorry. It's just—"

I could go on and on about the bullshit dissertation that wasn't getting written, my long, boring days marching back and forth in front of the bank, my falling out with Neil, the burden of dealing with everyone who suddenly had a stake in Billy's memorial service, my lingering guilt over Billy's death, but, really, they were all just excuses. The truth was that I'd let myself drift for far too long. The truth was that I'd always taken the easy way out. The truth was that it was my own damn fault that I'd fallen into the steep and irredeemable slump that defined the last few months. What scared me, though, was the possibility that I'd never hit bottom—and the fact that I had no idea what to do in the unlikely event that I did.

"You're right," I said, catching myself before I could manufacture a new set of excuses. "I'll work on it. I promise."

CHAPTER FIFTEEN

Frank lived less than two miles away from me, but where the world I lived in rang with the constant clatter of passing trains and tractor-trailers, Frank's smelled of woodsmoke and the sweet autumn incense of fallen oak leaves—even in June, when the trees that lined his narrow street were full and round with thick, green foliage. His was a world of stone houses and slate roofs, a country of carports and closed-in porches, a land of multiple chimneys and three-car garages. There were no sidewalks in Frank's neighborhood, just long macadam driveways lined with tall, narrow evergreens. A hammock swung idly in every backyard, and pitchers of lemonade sweated on kitchen windowsills as beagles romped over manicured lawns.

"How much do you want to bet he has a gardener?" I whispered as Karen and I walked the cobblestone path to Frank's front door. "I'll bet you anything that I could measure every blade of grass on this property and they'd all be the exact same length."

"I'm sure you could," Karen said, carrying the cherry pie she'd spent the afternoon baking. "But I was planning to enjoy a civilized dinner with rational human beings."

Letting the comment go, I knocked on Frank's door, and an African American woman invited us inside. Typical Frank, I thought as the woman took the pie from Karen and told us to make ourselves comfortable in what she called the sitting room. I didn't doubt for a second that he considered himself one hell of a guy for hiring minorities to take care of his household. I could just picture him counting the silverware every weekend to make sure none of it had been stolen, or patting himself on the back as he opened his swimming pool to his servants' families every year on the last day of summer, safe in the knowledge that he and his wife wouldn't be setting foot in the water until the following Memorial Day—and even then only after shocking the pool with enough chlorine to kill a whale.

A pair of French windows in Frank's sitting room looked out onto a flagstone patio, and a profusion of shrubs, cacti, ferns, and bonsai trees contributed to the illusion that there was no difference between inside and out. A baby grand piano sat in one corner of the room, artfully overrun with the vines of a philodendron, and a small fountain gurgled in the opposite corner.

"Sitting room," I muttered. "There's nowhere to sit. Unless, of course, you have a predilection for cactus needles."

"Predilection," Frank said, appearing in one of two doorways that opened onto the room. "There's an SAT word if I ever heard one. Not that I'd know. Dad paid someone to take the test for me. That's the rumor, anyway. Isn't it, Schwartz?"

My jaw moved silently as Frank extended a hand to Karen. Soft jazz played on miniature speakers concealed in the flowerpots. A muted guitar. A violin and oboe. Was this klezmer music, I wondered? Was this a shot at my alleged heritage?

"You must be the better half," Frank said to Karen. "Or in Charley's case, the better three-quarters. I take it you've met Maya?"

"No," I said. "Just the maid."

"Maid?" Frank said.

A second too late, Karen nudged me with her elbow and nodded in the direction of a wedding photo hanging on the wall just past the piano—Frank and the woman who had taken our pie.

"Shit," I whispered.

What more could I say? The most racist asshole I'd ever known had gone and married a black woman. Which didn't make him any less of an asshole, I told myself. Just less of a racist. And even then, just marginally so. In fact, I wouldn't have been the least bit surprised to learn that Frank had married Maya just to make me look bad.

"I'm Jewish," I blurted when Maya appeared in the doorway behind Frank. She was carrying a tray of hors d'oeuvres, and I rushed forward to take it from her. "I mean, I'm not Jewish. Not exactly, anyway, but Frank always thought I was. And, of course, I've always admired the Jews. And African Americans, too. Asians. Native Americans. On the whole, I'm very sensitive to the wants and needs of minorities in general."

Maya raised an eyebrow as I wrestled the tray from her hands.

"Please," I said. "Let me help you with that."

And then, in the ultimate act of betrayal, my cell phone went off, filling Frank and Maya's sitting room with a tinny version of the theme from *The Jeffersons*. We were moving on up to the East Side, the choir sang, to a deluxe apartment in the sky—where fish didn't fry in the kitchen and beans didn't burn on the grill. Yes, it took a whole lot of trying just to get up that hill, but now we were playing in the big leagues and getting our turn at bat. In short, we were finally getting a piece of the pie.

"I'm not a racist," I said as Karen shook her head in a vain attempt to shut me up. "If anyone's a racist, it's Frank. You should have heard the shit he used to say back at the Academy. Tell her, Frank. Tell her what you said the first time you saw Dwayne Coleman—about how you thought the school was segregated. Do you remember that, Frank? Do you remember saying that?"

"That's nothing," Maya said lightly. "You should have heard the line he used on me the night we met."

I looked at Karen, and we both looked at Maya.

"That was a joke," she said.

I let out a long sigh, and the knots in my back and shoulders started to relax.

"You okay, big guy?" Frank asked. "Can we get you anything? Water? Whiskey? A sedative?"

"I'm sorry," I said. "I don't know what I was thinking."

"You were thinking I was still sixteen years old," Frank said. "People do change, you know."

There was a distinct note of condescension in his voice, as if it were better to have been a racist and given it up than never to have been one at all, but I let it slide. The last thing I wanted was a prolonged discussion about who had changed the most since high school.

Over dinner, we sat at one end of a long, oak table in Frank's dining room. Candles were lit, and the lights were dimmed. A bittersweet combination of cinnamon and orange scents wafted through the air, and I could tell that Karen was being taken in by the rustic décor: handwoven rugs, hardwood floors, wicker baskets and wine-colored drapes. When she said the house was beautiful, I knew I'd lost her. Not for good, of course. But at least for the evening, and perhaps for the foreseeable future. Chances were pretty good that for the next few weeks Karen would be compelled to page through volumes and volumes of home furnishing catalogues to find every stick of furniture Frank and Maya owned.

As if I cared. As if I'd be the slightest bit impressed by the fact that Frank had an ottoman that cost roughly the same amount of money I made in a month or a china cabinet valued only slightly higher than my car. Please. Karen would talk about how comfortable their house was, how warm and inviting. She'd say she was just looking through the catalogues for decorating ideas, but I'd know what she was getting at even if she didn't.

My paycheck was inadequate.

I wasn't the man she needed me to be.

"I'm still trying to wrap my mind around this Billy Chin situation," Frank said, serving himself salad from a large wooden bowl. "Do you remember how happy he used to be? How we all used to mess with each other?"

Be Neil, I thought to myself. *Be Neil. Be Neil. Be Neil.*

"Yeah," I said. "Those were really good times."

"Like the time you said that thing about his haircut?"

"What thing about his haircut?" I asked. "What are you talking about?"

"Something about how he must have cut his hair with a sharp rock?"

Be Neil. Be Neil. Be Neil. Be Neil.

"I'm not sure," I said. "Is there any chance it was someone else?"

"I don't think so," Frank said. "I'm pretty sure it was you."

"I'm pretty sure it wasn't," I said.

"Really?" Frank said. "You don't remember? All of us taking shots at his haircut? And Billy was all, 'What's wrong with my haircut?' And you were like, 'Seriously, Billy? You look like you cut it with a sharp rock or something.' Classic, man. The whole room was in stitches."

"That never happened," I said.

"Are you kidding?" Frank asked. "Of course it happened."

"No," I said, vaguely aware that Karen was squeezing my knee under the table. "It didn't."

Be Neil. Be Neil. Be Neil. Be Neil.

"I'm pretty sure it did," Frank insisted.

Be Neil. Be Neil. Be Neil. Be—fuck it.

"I don't care what you remember, Frank," I said. "I'm telling you it didn't happen. And if you don't like it, then maybe you should go fuck yourself."

I regretted the words as soon as they were out of my mouth—not so much because they insulted Frank but because they made me look like an asshole.

Maya cleared her throat and asked Frank to pass a pitcher of water.

Frank passed the water and asked Karen what she thought of the salad.

Karen said that the salad was delicious and told Maya that she loved her necklace.

ALL THROUGH the main course and then through dessert, Maya and Karen kept the conversation on an even keel with talk of their jobs, their favorite movies, and whatever else people talk about when they have nothing in common. When I wasn't complimenting Maya's prowess in the kitchen only to find out that Frank had done the lion's share of cooking, I was making noises deep in my throat to suggest that I agreed with everything that everyone was saying—if only to prove that I knew how to behave in polite society. But when Frank offered to give us a tour of the house, I declined. It was a school night, I told him, and I'd already stayed up way past my bedtime. Though Karen agreed, she promised to give Maya a call so they could meet for lunch sometime. When Maya said it sounded like a great idea, all I could envision was an eternity of dinner parties at Frank's house, the four of us growing older and older with each passing year, with nothing but idle chatter and half-remembered lies about our days at the Academy to fill the silence between us. And when Karen and Maya went so far as to hug each other before saying goodbye, I knew my fate was sealed.

"Lunch?" I said as the Dearborns waved to us from their front step. "What were you thinking?"

I looked in my rearview mirror and cursed Frank as I pulled out of his driveway.

"They're not *that* bad," Karen said.

"Maybe *she* isn't," I said. "But *he* sure as hell is. And to tell you the truth, I'm not all that sure about her either.

I wouldn't be surprised if she works for Dow Chemical or something—developing a new improved formula for napalm."

"She teaches kindergarten," Karen said. "You'd know that if you'd been paying attention."

"Oh, and I'm sure she invites her entire class over to the house all the time. *Would you like the grand tour?* Please. As if we don't already know their house is bigger than ours."

"It's what people do, Charley. They show other people their homes. It's called being polite."

"Right," I said. "Polite. They were politely rubbing our noses in the fact that we're poor."

"We're not poor, Charley."

"We're not rich either."

"Since when has that mattered?"

"It doesn't." I snapped the radio on and off, and we drove for a while in silence—out of Frank's neighborhood and through the narrow tunnel that led under the railroad tracks separating my world from his. *The wrong side of the tracks*, I though glumly. Even my failures were shot through with clichés. "I just wish I were doing something with my life."

"You'll hit your stride. Once you finish your dissertation—"

"Sure," I said. "My dissertation. Like that's going anywhere."

"Give it some time," Karen said.

"Time," I said. "I've had all the time in the world, and where has it gotten me? Did I tell you I went down to the bridge where Billy killed himself?"

"No," Karen said. "You didn't. You don't tell me much of anything lately."

"Well, I did," I said. "I looked right over the edge and saw everything he saw. And for a second there, I understood why he did it. Only for a second, though. But long enough."

"Long enough for what?" Karen asked.

I turned onto our street and pretended not to hear my wife's question as the gravel popped under our tires.

"Charley, please. Long enough for what?"

"Long enough to know I could never do it," I said, cutting the engine. "Jump, I mean. I don't have it in me."

I opened my door, but Karen stayed still.

"Are you coming?" I asked.

"I don't like when you get this way, Charley."

"I know," I said. "I'm sorry."

"How can you just say that to me? How can you just tell me that you nearly killed yourself and decided at the last second that you couldn't do it?"

"Nearly killed myself?" I said. "That's not what I was saying at all."

"Then what were you saying?"

"I was saying that I took a ride to the Henry Avenue Bridge. I was saying that I looked over the edge. I was saying that I knew how Billy felt. But I was also saying that I couldn't do that—that I couldn't jump. That was my whole point. I would never do something like that."

"Okay," Karen said quietly. "But I want you to talk with someone about this. It doesn't have to be me, and it doesn't have to be a professional. But you really need to talk to someone. Neil, maybe. Or Dwayne, or Sean. Hell, talk to Greg Packer if it helps, but talk to *someone*, Charley. I mean it. Something's eating you up inside, and I hate seeing you so miserable."

"I know," I said again. And again, "I'm sorry."

Karen leaned over the gearshift and kissed me on the cheek. Her lips were soft and warm in the cool night air. I was a good man, she said. That was why she married me.

All she wanted was for me to be happy.

❦ CHAPTER SIXTEEN ❧

The minivan pulled into the parking lot at noon. It was a boxy Plymouth Voyager with wood trim and tinted windows. The driver wore tight jeans and a white tee shirt, and she gave me a wave as she stepped from the vehicle. Or not a wave so much as a quick glance over the frames of her sunglasses as she raised a finger to indicate that she'd be with me in a second. Then she turned back to the minivan, and I knew I was screwed. Inside, I could see five shadowy figures trying their best to strangle each other in the cargo hold; and though I tried to back away as the woman reached for the silver handle of the sliding door, my costume was too bulky and my range of motion far too restricted for me to make even a respectable attempt at retreat.

Tumbling from the vehicle in a chaotic tangle of bright yellow soccer jerseys, heavy cleats, and shin guards, the kids saw me immediately and made a beeline for my balloons. My guess as the earth shook beneath me was that I had approximately three seconds to live, and when the pushing started, I toppled right over.

My first instinct was to let go of the balloons, but I'd tied them to my wrist on the advice of Sue and the guy who smelled like sausage. In theory, it was good advice, but in the real world, it only gave my assailants something to fight for, so three of them started kicking me with their hard, heavy, hateful cleats, and the other two yanked so violently on the balloons that my hand turned five shades of purple.

So this was my life, I thought glumly, wondering where it had all gone wrong as the sprinklers came on and the kids skittered away. When I was four years old, my mother used to warn me against doing anything dangerous by telling me that if I got killed, she'd have to put me in a box and bury me underground. Now here I was, sinking into the muddy lawn in front of the bank inside my giant dollar sign, and it wasn't because of anything I'd done. In fact, with the striking exception of asking Karen to marry me, I couldn't think of a single thing that I'd actually *done* since graduating from the Academy. College, sure, but even graduating with honors was more a matter of figuring out which classes would require the least amount of work than of cracking open the occasional book and learning something. Even grad school was nothing more than an attempt at escaping the real world after two years of bouncing from job to job in quasi-corporate America. Temping, editing, proofreading. Before Billy, I used to joke that I'd rather hang myself than line edit another accounting textbook—by way of an explanation for quitting my last job, by way of justifying my choice to return to school, by way of insisting that I wasn't a failure. I was moving up, I was trying to say. I was taking charge. I was plotting a course to a better future. But really I was only taking the path of least resistance. The only good thing—the only real thing—that came as a result of grad school was meeting Karen. Now I was floundering with my dissertation and, if I really wanted to be honest with myself, floundering in my marriage as well. All because of my aversion to work. All because I refused to *do* anything.

Because doing something meant change.

Because change meant growing up.

Because growing up meant leaving so much behind.

Phil Ennis was only half-right when he said that I thought my hands were clean because I was a cynic. The real truth was the reverse of that: I wore a cynical mask to keep myself from getting too attached to anything, to protect myself from getting too involved, to distance myself from the living because in the end I knew the only thing that separated them from the dead was time and that everyone I loved would one day be gone. So I learned to turn everything into a joke—my friends, my job, my house, my life— and when Billy died, the joke stopped being funny.

This was no way for an adult to live, I told myself as the sprinklers cut off and I heard a fresh set of footsteps squishing across the lawn. And it wasn't enough to be Neil or the replacement Neil or whoever it was I'd been trying to be since Neil got pissed at me for sending the wrong letter to Ennis. What I needed to do was stand on my own two feet. What I needed to do was learn to be me.

Whoever that was.

"We've put this off long enough, Charley," Sue said, huffing and puffing as she made her way across the lawn.

THE PERFORMANCE review was not designed to penalize employees, Sue said mechanically, as if reading from a script. Rather, I should view it as an opportunity to assess my strengths and weaknesses in a way that would make me a greater asset to the company. Ideally, it would open up a dialogue between myself and management that would ultimately lead to advancement within my profession, but it might also give me an opportunity to assess whether my current career path was right for me.

"At the moment, I'm curled into a ball inside of a giant dollar sign," I said, in case she hadn't noticed. "I'm not sure that counts as a career path."

"Just play along, Charley," Sue said. "I need to do this for everyone. What would you describe as your towering strengths?"

"Towering strengths?" I said.

"Things you're especially good at."

"I understand the question," I said. "I just wasn't prepared for it. I thought the whole point of this was for you to tell me what I was doing wrong."

"It is," Sue said. "But it's supposed to be a dialogue. I ask you a few questions, you give me a few answers, I tell you why you're wrong, and we pretend we had a real conversation about your value to the company."

"Are you this forthcoming with all your employees?"

"No," Sue said. "Only the ones who are lying in mud. What do you see as your towering strengths?"

"I don't know," I said. "I guess I'm good at holding onto my balloons."

"Okay," Sue said, and she made a note on the clipboard. "Weaknesses?"

"Pretty much everything else," I said.

"Could you be more specific?" Sue asked.

"I'm sure I could," I said. "How much time do you have?"

Sue looked at her watch, and I told her not to worry. The job wasn't right for me, I said. In fact, it probably wasn't right for anyone—anyone with any self-respect, anyway. Or job skills of any kind.

"No offense," I added, untying my balloons and shimmying out of the dollar sign. "But this is ridiculous."

"So, what?" Sue asked. "You're quitting on me?"

"It looks that way," I said. "I just hope my wife doesn't kill me for it."

It wasn't the same as all the other times, I told myself as I dragged the dollar sign back to the bank and shoved it into the broom closet looking scuffed, dirty, and bald in places where time and bad luck had rubbed away its glitter.

I was quitting, yes. But quitting with a purpose.

❧ CHAPTER SEVENTEEN ☙

The recipe called for two boned chicken breasts, an assortment of vegetables, and a splash of lemon juice. How hard could it be, I wondered? Chop the veggies, lay them on the chicken, add the lemon, wrap the whole she-bang in foil, and stick it in the oven. With any luck, the end result would be a romantic dinner for two that would at least begin to make up for the fact that I'd quit my job. That four days had passed since I'd done the deed was beside the point. What mattered now was the element of surprise. If I timed everything right, Karen would walk through the door just as I was lighting the candles; but even if the meal went bust, the gesture alone would be so unexpected, so overwhelmingly out of character, that my wife would be speechless—in a good way, for a change.

It was Thursday afternoon, nearly a week since I told Karen about my visit to the Henry Avenue Bridge. For Karen, it was a week lost to grading end-of-semester research papers, creative writing portfolios, and final exams. For me, it was a week of answering the phone and agreeing to whatever crass and misguided schemes my fellow Academy grads had cooked up for turning Billy's memorial service into the social event of the season. But if a circus was what they wanted, I thought, chopping peppers into tiny squares as the telephone rang, then a circus was what they'd get.

"Hey," Neil said when I picked up the phone. "It's me."

"I'm chopping peppers," I said, cradling the receiver between my ear and my shoulder. "Red and green. Dangerous stuff, so this better be good."

"Did you get my message?"

"Oh, right," I said. "Greg. I meant to call you back."

"You gave him a ride to the airport?"

"Sorry," I said. "It seemed like a good idea at the time."

Neil let out a sigh. He sounded tired, and suddenly I felt bad for all the times I called him away from his job, away from his family, away from his life to help me pretend that I'd never have to grow up if I didn't feel like it.

"You okay?" I said.

"He was arrested," Neil said. "Greg, I mean. Apparently he went apeshit on his mother. Nothing physical, thank God, but they were out shopping, and he started screaming at her for sabotaging his life."

"He told you this?" I said.

"In his own way, of course. In his version, he's the hero, and it was all a misunderstanding."

"So, what?" I scraped the peppers off the cutting board and onto the foil with the chicken and the other vegetables. "His mother called the cops?"

"Worse. They were in the grocery store when it happened, so it turned into a big to-do. The manager called the cops, and the cops hauled Greg away for disturbing the peace. They let him go when his mom came down to the station to make a statement, but by then? Jesus, the guy's out of control. Sullivan's still pushing for an intervention, but part of me thinks he just likes the drama."

"Does Sean have experience with this kind of thing?" I asked.

"Not exactly," Neil said. "I think he picked up a pamphlet at work."

"The car lot or the other job?"

"To tell you the truth, I don't even know."

I put the chicken in the oven and told Neil it was his call. If he wanted to give Sullivan a shot and go ahead with an intervention, however loosely we used the term, then I'd back him all the way. But if he wanted to wash his hands of the entire situation, I'd understand completely. There was only so much Packer anyone could take, and Neil had already endured far more than I'd have guessed was humanly possible.

"Thanks," Neil said. "I'll let you know what I decide."

I said goodbye to Neil and dimmed the lights in the dining room by standing on a chair and unscrewing two of the bulbs in the faux-brass fixture attached to the ceiling fan. Then I lit some candles and fluffed some sticky brown rice with a fork per the instructions on the package. In addition to the vegetables I'd chopped, I also steamed some spinach in compliance with Karen's firm belief that vegetables cooked with meat products were not so much vegetables but a kind of garnish. Though I normally disagreed with this theory, I decided to acquiesce in the spirit of romance. As an added touch, I put on a jacket and tie and slicked my hair back so I'd look my best when Karen walked in the door. Since she was due back any minute, there was a slight element of haste as I selected music for the evening and filled a Rubbermaid bucket with ice to keep our wine cool while we dined. I was uncorking the bottle when I heard a knock at the door.

Odd, I thought, because I was certain that Karen had a key.

Or not so odd, I realized when I saw it wasn't Karen at the door but Sean Sullivan.

"I told Neil we should have done this a long time ago," he said, brushing past me as I opened the door. "But he put it off and put it off, and now look. The police are involved. Greg has a criminal record. We all saw it coming, but did we lift a finger to stop it? No. We just sat back and laughed while Greg screwed up his life. Greg's stalking a girl in Chicago? Oh, boy! What fun! Greg's hooked on painkillers? What a character! I'm telling you, Charley, it's only a matter of time before we turn on the news and find out that some nut strangled his mother in the Christmas room. Then they'll start interviewing his friends, and every one of us will be on TV saying, gee, he seemed like such a nice guy, I have no idea what happened. We'll be *those* people, Charley. Those people who never have a clue that their neighbor has fifty prostitutes tied up in the basement. You see them on the news all the time and think, God, they must have been dumb as rocks not to realize their neighbor was a psychopath, and that's what people are going to say about us!"

He stopped to catch his breath and asked what the candles were for.

"Romantic dinner," I said. "For two."

The telephone rang, and when I answered, it was Neil calling to inform me that he'd made a decision regarding the Greg Packer situation. He was going ahead with the intervention, he said. Since my house was centrally located, he told everyone to meet there.

"Everyone?" I said.

"Sean and Dwayne. Anthony can't make it, but he said he'd stay up for the evening news to see if any of us gets killed."

There was another knock, and Sean opened the door for Dwayne. Neil said he was calling from his car and would be at my house in less than an hour. He hoped he wasn't imposing, he said, and I hurried into the kitchen to remove the chicken from the oven.

"No, not at all," I said.

Karen's key turned in the lock, and I cursed out loud as steam escaped from the foil and burned my fingers. There was some mumbling in the living room as Sean and Dwayne tried to explain what they were doing there, but the only words I could discern were *Charley*, *Greg Packer*, *kitchen*, and *romantic dinner*.

"Hi, honey," I said as Karen peered cautiously into the kitchen. "Surprise."

℘ CHAPTER EIGHTEEN ℘

Over a dinner consisting of two chicken breasts split five ways, Sean outlined the game plan. We'd show up at Greg's house and invite him out for a friendly night on the town. Very casual, Sean explained. The key was to make it sound like a fun evening out with the guys at the restaurant of his choice. We weren't going to lie to Greg, of course, and the second we all sat down and placed our orders, Neil would tell him in no uncertain terms that the reason we were meeting with him was to voice our collective concern that his grasp on reality was tenuous at best.

We were not to raise our voices, Sean said as if our original plan had been to kick Greg's door in, wrap him in duct tape, and drive all night until we found a nuthouse that was crazy enough to take him in. And we were not to level accusations. We were simply to state facts.

"So, this is what?" I said as we all piled into Dwayne's Toyota. "About the drinking? The pills? The fight with his mother?"

"Take your pick," Dwayne said.

"But an intervention is usually about a single issue, right?"

"Not necessarily," Sean said, scanning his pamphlet for evidence to support his case.

I looked to Neil for a sign of affirmation, a shrug that said yes, I was right, but that tonight was Sean's moment to shine, his chance to show us all that we could take him seriously, that three years of grad school weren't for nothing, and that, above all, we respected him enough to let him take charge. Instead, Neil avoided my gaze as he picked up his cell phone and called Greg to inform him that we were all in the neighborhood and were hoping to meet him for dinner.

"One last question," I said after Neil ended the call. "What happens if we actually convince Greg that he needs help?"

"What do you mean?" Sean said.

"Aren't we supposed to take him somewhere?"

"I hadn't really thought about that," Sean said. "But I'm sure we can work something out."

"We can still do the forcible commitment," Dwayne suggested. "Get him in the car and head straight for Philly. If the bastard gets violent, I break out the pepper spray. Easy as pie."

"It won't come to that," Neil said.

"So you say."

"We'll be in a public place."

"Didn't stop him last time."

"He'll be fine," Neil said. "No pepper spray."

I waited for a joke, a line from the Marx Brothers, but all Neil did was bite the hair on the back of his hand as Dwayne wove in and out of traffic.

<hr />

"Remember," Sean said as Neil rang Greg's doorbell. "Nice and casual."

"Right," I said, jerking a thumb at Dwayne. "That's why we brought the police."

Greg's mother opened the door, and her eyes went wide with delight. It had been years, she sang, since she'd been called upon by so many handsome young suitors.

"Mother!" Greg shouted from somewhere upstairs. "Stop playing the strumpet and show my associates up to my living quarters."

"His majesty beckons," Dwayne muttered.

"He's angry at me because I took back my Christmas room," Greg's mother whispered, covering her mouth with four fingers to suggest that she'd gotten away with something naughty. "But I don't care. It's *my* Christmas room, not his base of operations or whatever he calls it."

"My *war room*, mother!" Greg bellowed. "*It's my war room!*"

Greg's mother rolled her eyes as her son glowered down at her from the top of the steps in full Nazi regalia. Decked out in a spiked helmet, gray topcoat, and black leather jackboots, he explained that Anthony Gambacorta knew a guy who knew a guy who sold, traded, and collected Nazi memorabilia.

"Rifles, daggers, medals, uniforms," Greg said as he descended the stairway and the steps creaked under his weight. "The topcoat and helmet are genuine. As are most of the props that Anthony intends to employ in the production."

Apparently we wouldn't be visiting Greg's living quarters, I thought as his mother gushed about how dashing he looked in uniform and, again, how lucky she was to be surrounded by so many striking young men.

"My friends are far from striking, Mother," Greg huffed, herding us out the door. "They're average at best. But as we all know, beggars can't be choosers, so, if you don't mind, I'll bid you adieu until morning."

"The regular breakfast?" his mother asked.

"Yes," Greg said. "The regular breakfast."

"Toast?"

Greg paused in the doorway, the spike of his helmet giving his gray silhouette the contours of a Christmas tree.

"White," he said and pulled the door shut behind him. "I apologize, gentlemen, for that embarrassing display of emotion. Mother clearly needs to get out more."

"She's not the only one," Dwayne said. "Would you take that goddamn teakettle off your head? It's embarrassing."

"It's hardly a teakettle," Greg said. "It's a vintage Wehrmacht Pickelhaube."

"I don't care what it is," Dwayne said. "You're not wearing it in my car. It'll tear the hell out of my ceiling."

"I'm sorry," Greg said. "But I need to stay in character until curtain call."

"That's fair," Sean said, clutching his pamphlet. "Isn't that fair, guys?"

"Christ," Dwayne said. "You expect me to drive around with a Nazi all night?"

"I acknowledge your consternation," Greg said. "But I can assure you that I'm no Nazi. Rather, I'm playing the role of a Nazi in a stage production set behind enemy lines at the height of the Second World War."

"Do you always have to talk down to me?" Dwayne said.

"Talk down to you?" Greg said. "I'm merely explaining the art of theater."

"Well, art is art, isn't it?" Neil said, quickly stepping between Dwayne and Greg before their exchange could escalate into the realm of the physical. "Still, on the other hand, water is water. And east is east, and west is west, and if you take cranberries and stew them like applesauce they taste much more like prunes than rhubarb does."

Duck Soup? I wondered.

"Whatever," Dwayne said, shaking his head as he unlocked his car. "Wear the damn helmet. I don't care. But you're sitting in the back with Schwartz and Sullivan."

It could have been worse, I told myself as the bulk of Greg's body pressed against me like a parade float. Instead of *Down in the Stalag,* Greg could have been starring in an all-nude production of *Hung Jury* and I wouldn't have had the heavy wool of his gray topcoat to save me from getting lost in the doughy folds of his gut.

WHEN WE arrived at the Wednesday Club on Route 611, the hostess took one look at Greg and sat our party in a dimly lit corner of the restaurant, far from anyone who might, for whatever reason, find his sartorial preferences offensive.

"I wonder if we'll have the same waitress as last time," Greg said as he lowered himself onto his seat. "I think she had a thing for me."

"Last time?" Dwayne said. "What the hell are you talking about?"

"When we met to raise money for Billy," Greg said.

"That was a different restaurant altogether," Dwayne said, though, to be fair to Greg, both establishments had the same rusty street signs, the same ads for motor oil, the same fading sports memorabilia, the same banged-up musical instruments, the same sleds and bikes and hammers and saws, the same photos of dead celebrities, and the same nostalgic vibe as every chain up and down the Pennsylvania Turnpike. "How the hell could we possibly end up with the same waitress?"

"Keep it casual," Sean wheezed, trying desperately to sound as if he were clearing his throat. "Nice and casual."

"Nice and casual my ass," Dwayne said. "I'm sick of this bullshit. Greg, the reason we brought you here tonight is that we think you're off your rocker, okay? A total fucking nut job."

"I see," Greg said. "Should we order a pitcher of beer?"

"I'm not sure that's the best of ideas," Neil said as Sean unfolded his pamphlet to see what our next move should be. "The thing is, Greg, you've been acting a little strange over the past few months, and we're worried about where you're going to end up."

"We're not here to level accusations," Sean said, glancing at his pamphlet. "We're only here to talk."

"So this is what?" Greg said. "Some kind of intervention?"

Before anyone could answer, the waitress came to take our drink order, and Greg instructed her to bring a pitcher of sweetened iced tea with a twist of lemon and to leave it without further comment. Five minutes later, he said, she was to return to take our orders for supper. Thinking ahead, he speculated that he might be in the mood for meat loaf, but he couldn't be sure, so it would be best if she checked with him before placing the order. We were apparently in the middle of an intervention, Greg explained officiously, so it was important that she follow his every command to the letter. Otherwise, said intervention might not work.

The waitress nodded and left us alone.

"See, Greg, there's part of the problem," Neil said. "You're always bossing people around."

"You say that as if you want our waitress intruding on our privacy every five seconds," Greg said. "I'm only trying to expedite the healing process, if you don't mind. I'm starring in a musical a few days from now, and I need to work on my lines. By the way, Charley, would it bother you too much if I spoke in a German accent while we discussed my mental health? Given your heritage, you're perfectly within your rights to stop me."

I looked up from my menu.

"Maybe a pitcher of beer isn't a bad idea," I said.

"Fine," Greg said, signaling the waitress. "But there's still the issue of your Jewish heritage to consider."

"I'm not Jewish," I said. "Not that it should matter."

"My sources say otherwise," Greg said. And then to the waitress, "A pitcher of your finest ale, please."

Two pitchers of the Wednesday Club's finest ale later, we were picking at the greasy remains of burgers and fries as Greg rambled on about the eternal battle between good and evil, the peculiar relationship between mothers and sons, and his need to procure an heir at all costs.

"Have you thought about maybe getting a job first?" Dwayne asked.

"Don't be ridiculous," Greg said. "My goal is to find a woman who's either independently wealthy or gainfully employed. I'd prefer the former, of course, but I'm more than willing to settle for the latter. Needless to say, money isn't my only criterion, but it *is* an important one. I'm also considering such variables as teeth, hips, posture, finger-nails, and, in the event of a tie, bosoms. They don't have to be big, but they have to be firm. By the way, Charley, did you ever mention my proposal to Karen?"

"Can we please not bring my wife into this?" I said.

"Frankly, I'm disappointed that she didn't take part in tonight's proceedings. A woman's touch is exactly what this intervention is missing—the efforts of our buxom waitress notwithstanding."

"And I thought Charley was nuts," Dwayne muttered.

"What?" I said.

"What do you mean *what*?" Dwayne said. "That whole episode on the bridge."

"What episode?" Sean asked. "Did I miss something?"

"No," I said.

"Our buddy here decided to take a field trip down to the bridge where Billy killed himself," Dwayne said.

"Allegedly killed himself," Greg corrected him.

"Fuck *allegedly*," Dwayne said. "The bastard jumped." He wasn't even drinking.

"That's hardly appropriate," Greg said. "Given the circum-stances."

"I don't believe it," Sean said. "You went to the bridge, and you didn't invite me?"

"It wasn't exactly a good time," Neil said.

"Schwartz nearly killed himself," Dwayne said. "I had to wrestle him to the ground."

"That's not what happened," I said. "That's not what happened at all."

"Given the details you've just related, I find it more than a little curious that I'm the target of this evening's intervention," Greg said, emptying our second pitcher. "Perhaps next time we should all show up at Charley's house unannounced. He clearly needs more counseling than I do. Who's up for more beer?"

"I wasn't going to do it," I said. "I was never going to jump."

"Could have fooled me," Dwayne said.

"I wasn't," I said.

"Okay," Neil said. "Let's all take a breath."

"I don't see why that's necessary," Greg said. "Especially when all of the evidence would suggest that Charley's the one who's unhinged."

"I'm not unhinged," I said, looking to Neil for confirmation. "Right? I mean, *you* were there. I wasn't going to jump, was I?"

"Let's focus on Greg," Neil said.

"You think I wanted to jump?"

"I don't know," Neil said. "I was trying to hold my lunch down."

"Why the hell would I do something like that?"

"Why did Billy do it?" Dwayne asked.

"He was in a bad place," I said.

I didn't need to think about it anymore. The phrase came automatically.

"Well, the good news, gentlemen, is that I'm not in a bad place at all," Greg said. "In fact, I'm in a very good place. Life with mother is no bed of roses, but I have *Down in the Stalag* to look forward to. After that, who knows? Hollywood? Broadway? Briefly, to be sure, but long enough to make a name for myself and, above all, to meet and marry the woman of my dreams."

"You're right, Greg," Dwayne said. "You're definitely in a good place. A sane place? No fucking way. But a good place nonetheless. An awesome, wonderful, glorious, fan-damn-tastic Nirvana of a place, and I hope you like living there because I'm done trying to pull you out of it."

Dwayne signaled the waitress and asked for the check.

"But we're not done here," Sean said, scanning his pamphlet, apparently for information on what do when an intervention goes south. "We still need to—"

Neil raised a discreet hand and shook his head. The check would be fine, he told the waitress when she paused at our table. After we dropped Greg off at his house, Sean suggested we find an all-night diner where we could grab a cup of coffee and try to figure out where we went wrong.

"Where *we* went wrong?" Dwayne demanded. "I don't know about you guys, but I sure as hell wasn't invited to the conception."

"I'm just saying it would be good for next time if we could figure out what to do differently."

"Next time?" Dwayne said. "Please. Unless we're luring him into Philly, you can count me out."

"He'll be at the memorial service," I suggested. "You could haul him in then."

"No one's getting hauled in," Neil said quietly. "Greg has to do this on his own."

"Do what, exactly?" Dwayne asked.

"I wish I knew," Neil said.

No one spoke for the rest of the drive. When we arrived at my house, Dwayne barely paused long enough for the rest of us to jump out of his car. He'd see us at the memorial service, he said before speeding away.

"So," I said, as Sean ducked into his own car and followed suit.

"So," Neil said.

We sat on my porch in the warm June air as a train rattled by and the cars and trucks hummed along Route 30.

"Do you ever get the feeling that no matter what you do, nothing's going to work out the way you want it to?" Neil said.

"All the time," I said.

"Like all you want is to fix everything, but the harder you try, the worse it gets."

"This isn't about Greg, is it?"

"I've been offered a job in DC," Neil said. "Health and Human Services."

"I guess this is it, then. The end of the road."

"Give me a break," Neil said. "I'm getting the same static from my mom. She told me yesterday she had to take the knobs off the stove to keep dad from burning the house down. She thinks I'm leaving because I don't want to deal with him."

"She's just scared," I said. "Believe me, I know how she feels. I've been trying to be you for the past week or so, but I don't think it's working."

"That's funny," Neil said. "Why would you want to be me?"

"Got tired of being me, I guess. That and you're the only sane friend I have."

Neil laughed. "Please. If I were sane, I'd shack up in Mrs. Packer's Christmas room and join the cast of *Down in the Stalag*."

"I know what you mean," I said. "There's something oddly attractive about that boy's life."

"He's so damn sure of himself."

"It's his model of the universe," I said. "You'd be sure of yourself, too, if you had it all figured out."

"That's the thing," Neil said. "Sometimes I think I do. It's just a matter of getting all the pieces to fit. The only problem is they never hold still. As soon as the puzzle's out of the box, you realize the pieces are all screwed up. Half of them don't even go together, and the ones that do start moving and changing and losing their minds before you can even start to figure out what's going on. You could force them, of course."

"But then you'd be Greg," I said.

"Yeah," Neil whispered. "Stone cold crazy."

"It's like that time on the two bus," I said. "Remember when the riot broke out?"

"Yeah," Neil said. "Clubs and chains and two-by-fours."

"And a knife, I think. Broomsticks and a soup ladle."

"Fist grabs broomstick," Neil said. "Broomstick sweeps pool cue."

"You just keep playing and hope the driver knows what he's doing."

"That's fine when you're a dumb kid," Neil said. "But what happens when you wake up one day and find yourself behind the wheel?"

"You open the door and let the crazies on," I said. "Or off, depending on what they want."

"Meanwhile the bus keeps moving," Neil said.

"It has to," I said. "Otherwise?"

"Otherwise," Neil said.

He left it at that, and we sat quietly as a pair of moths slapped the porch light above with an unsteady rhythm. It wasn't the end, I told myself. We'd always be friends. Yes, there would be distance, yes, there would be work and wives and probably children, and, yes, there would be long stretches of silence where neither of us would hear a peep from the other for months or maybe even years; but each of us would always know the other was out there somewhere, a phone call away, an email, a thought, a joke, a dream, making the world a more bearable place, divining some measure of sense from the chaos, laughing and crying in the same breath because neither is ever enough on its own and the alternative is to give up on the game altogether. As we sat on my porch, two men, not quite old, but no longer boys, I knew that Neil was my friend, and at the moment, it was all I needed.

Two days before Billy Chin's memorial service, Karen and I received separate invitations to see Greg perform in the world premiere of *Down in the Stalag*. Printed on heavy stock, the invitations made no mention of Billy whatsoever. They simply stated that Gloria Packer was pleased to announce that her son, Gregory James Packer III, would be starring as Sergeant Schlitz in the production. Certain words in the invitation were printed in block capital letters. GREGORY JAMES PACKER III, for example. STARRING and WORLD PREMIERE as well. Our kind attendance, the invitations informed us, would not be overlooked, and Karen's included a handwritten note from Greg's mother stating that she would be more than delighted if Karen would see fit to enjoy the musical seated next to her in a row reserved for friends and family.

When I called Neil to find out if he'd received an invitation as well, he told me that in addition to inviting every member of our graduating class, Greg's mother had invited anyone with whom Greg had come into contact over the past ten years. The list included (but was not limited to) aunts and uncles, college professors, women he'd met online, the doctor who prescribed his painkillers, a fourteen-year-old opera singer, a cadre of lesser-known conservative radio personalities, a retired professional wrestler named Crusher Helgstrom, the police officer who arrested Greg at the grocery store, and the Mayor of Philadelphia. Naturally, Greg was furious at his mother for meddling in his personal affairs, and he vowed that vengeance upon her would be swift and merciless.

"Sullivan's pressing for another intervention," Neil said.

"And you?"

"I don't know."

"We could make it a weekly event," I said. "Rotating cast. Celebrity guests for the February sweeps."

"Madeline would love that. We barely see each other as it is."

"You did what you could," I said.

"I told him to give it up—this thing with his mother, I mean. I told him to let it go. It's not healthy, I said. You're not getting anywhere."

"Sounds familiar."

"I can only say it so many times."

"Maybe it's time for you to let him go," I said. "It's his life. Let him live it."

"That's what Madeline says."

"That's what *everyone* says."

"She wants to know why I bother."

"Good question," I said.

An audible shrug. "I wish I knew."

"Listen," I said. "There's something I need to tell you. I really screwed things up between us."

"Don't mention it."

"No, it was stupid. I don't care what Ennis thinks. Or Frank Dearborn, or any of those guys."

"Yes, you do," Neil said.

"I know. But I wish I didn't."

"Let it go," Neil said. "Whatever you have against them, let it go."

"Right," I said. "As soon as you let Greg go."

"As soon as he lets this war with his mother go."

"Like that'll happen any time soon."

"We need to move on," Neil said.

"Yeah," I said. "I guess we do."

And I would have. Or might have. Conceivably. But then I saw Frank Dearborn on the morning of the memorial service, and it all came back to me—the anger, the fear, the panic, the doubt, the envy and self-pity. Who was I trying to kid? I didn't know a thing about Billy Chin. Yeah, we were friends, but only in the sense that we'd gone to the same school and hadn't managed to become enemies, only in the sense that we used to talk once in a while, only in the sense that his name never made it onto the ever-growing list of things that pissed me off. But beyond that?

I tried to conjure a picture of Billy in my mind, to reconstruct him with memories and anecdotes, but the best I could do as Karen and I got in the car and headed for the Academy that morning was to imagine a stick figure. Billy was skinny. He wore a blue suit. He played ping-pong and chess and was a member of the debate team. He ate rice for lunch and carried his books in a giant duffle bag. If I really thought about it, I could wrestle a few more details from the dim corners of my mind, but they were either too sketchy or tinged with regret to be of any use.

He scored summa cum laude on the National Latin Exam—or was I only making that up? He had an encyclopedic knowledge of breakfast cereal commercials from the 1980s—or was that someone else? He nearly threw up in biology lab when we first cut into our cat—or was that me?

"Are you okay?" Karen asked as we slowed to a stop at an intersection on the edge of the city. "You seem a little distracted."

"I'm fine," I said. "Just thinking about what I'll say at the service."

"You don't have anything prepared?"

"Of course I do," I lied, tapping my breast pocket as if my remarks were all mapped out and folded in quarters an inch away from my heart. "But I want to make sure I didn't forget anything."

If Karen said anything after that, I missed it.

Out of the corner of my eye, I could see the sleek, silver cat on the hood of Frank's Jaguar creeping over my shoulder and slinking discreetly but decisively into view. When I turned to get a better look, Frank leaned forward to peer past his wife and give me a wave. His roof was down, his hair windblown but stylish, his sunglasses worth more than the car I was driving.

"Asshole," I muttered.

"You *do* know our windows are open," Karen said.

"Fuck," I whispered, pounding the steering wheel. "Fuck, fuck, fuck, fuck, fuck."

"Charley?"

Why couldn't I have been nicer to him? Why couldn't I have been a better friend? Why couldn't I have returned his calls or answered his emails? We were supposed to be like brothers—that's what they always told us at the Academy. We were supposed to be a family. But all I had were a handful of vague memories of walking the halls with Billy and bitching about friends who didn't know how to be friends, about teachers who pissed me off, about bands that had sold out, and TV shows that had stopped being funny.

When the light in front of us turned green, Frank took off and was already half a block ahead of me when my cell phone went off, taunting me with strains of the theme from *The Jeffersons*. Letting out an aggrieved, rumbling sigh, I hit the gas, and my Saturn lurched forward in a tired approximation of hot pursuit.

"If he thinks he's getting to this thing before me," I said, and my voice trailed off as I jerked my steering wheel to the left to avoid slamming into a parked car.

"Why does it matter?" Karen asked, gripping her seatbelt.

"It matters," I said, though I knew it didn't.

In my head, at least, I knew it didn't matter. But in my gut, I had to beat Frank. Just once. Just to prove that I could. Sure, he had the better car, the better job, the better house, the better life, but if I could only make it to Billy's memorial service before Frank did, then maybe it would prove once and for all that I was the better friend.

Seriously, I thought as I pressed a heavy foot to the gas pedal—fuck Frank if he thought he could tell me what I did and didn't say to Billy about his haircut. Yeah, I took shots at him from time to time, but we all did, just like we all took shots at each other every chance we got. Because that was the whole point. That was the game and how it was played. You saw an opening and you took it. A failed test, a shitty car, an ugly tie, a festering pimple—even a bad haircut.

And, okay, what if I *did* ask Billy if he cut his hair with a sharp rock? It was funny because it was true. Compared to the moussed-up, slicked-back, butch-waxed, permanent press coifs we all used to wear back when we were kids, Billy's fine, black hair was a throwback to an age before hairspray. Not that he needed me to humiliate him over it, but what was the point of going to a prep school if not to be tortured day in and day out by your closest friends? And it wasn't just any prep school, either. It was *the Academy*, for Christ's sake. The best damn school in the history of the universe.

By the time I caught up with Frank, he was stopped at a light that was about to go green, so I used the opportunity to rocket past him and take the lead. It was early in the morning, and the street was dead. The few shops that were still in business in this part of the city specialized in rent-to-own kitchen appliances and secondhand furniture. All the others were closed for good, windows covered over with newspapers, plywood, or thin layers of soap. Karen begged me to slow down, but it was no use. It wasn't just Frank I was trying to outrun. It wasn't even the ghost of Billy Chin so much as the memories of all the shitty things I'd ever done to him.

Junior year, for example. It was the sixty-fifth anniversary of Elvis Presley's birth, and the tabloids had people sighting the King of Rock 'n' Roll all over the country. Given that I was a cocky seventeen-year-old asshole with a clunky video camera and a complete lack of respect for anything, I thought it would be funny to shoot a documentary-style movie about the King's return starring Billy as Elvis. The joke, I explained, would be that nobody would say a word about the fact that Elvis was a skinny Asian kid who played the flute. It wasn't until I finished running the plan by him that I realized I might as well have called him Rice Dick. His eyes drifted down toward his scuffed black shoes, and his skinny hands twitched at his sides. Was that how I saw him, the look on his face demanded? As the punch line to a joke?

But the joke wasn't on him, I wanted to say. It was on Elvis. Or his fans. Or all the people who believed he was coming back. That Billy played the flute was just the icing on the cake. Couldn't he see the humor in that? Elvis Presley returning from the grave as a flautist? A Chinese flautist, no less? Which, the more I thought about it, made me realize that the joke came back to the fact that Billy was Asian, so I dropped the whole subject and told him I was only messing around. Anyone who knew me was also aware of the fact that I'd never follow through with something so ambitious as a documentary, even a fake one, even one shot on my parents' VHS recorder. So what if I'd already written the script? So what if it called for Billy to deliver his lines like Charlie Chan? Did that mean I was a racist? Did it make me an asshole? Did it put me in the same league as Frank Dearborn?

I barreled past a public high school and a bright yellow sign warning me to watch out for children. The traffic was getting heavier now, the city more dense with bars and gas stations, so I took a sharp left and roared through the underpass that ran beneath the railroad tracks that cut a gash through the city like the stitches running up the length of Billy's wrist.

He was going back to school for computers, he said the last time I saw him. Because working as a pharmacist? The hours alone were enough to make him—

He shook his head but never finished the thought.

It was New Year's Eve. Everyone was there. Neil and Madeline. Dwayne Coleman and Sean Sullivan. Even Greg Packer, if only to hit on Karen, and Anthony Gambacorta to sabotage my cell phone. There was music. There was drinking. There were occasional snatches of something approaching wit. On television, there was the countdown, but the volume was low because the ball wouldn't drop for at least another hour. Beyond that, I couldn't remember.

I couldn't remember what song was playing.

I couldn't remember what food we served.

I couldn't remember what I was drinking or wearing or even what I was thinking when Billy told me that he was going back to school for computers.

All I could remember was what I said next:

Computers? Jesus, Billy, I'd rather be dead!

I wasn't being serious.

I didn't mean it literally.

I just meant that I could never learn code or sit at a computer for hours on end.

What I meant was more power to him, but it came out all wrong, so I laughed to let him know that I was really only kidding, and Billy half-laughed, half-smiled, half-looked at his wrist as if to check the time, as if to make sure I saw his stitches, and said that he was sorry but he had somewhere to be.

Could I have stopped him? Maybe.

Could I have insisted that he stick around? Sure.

But the point is I didn't, and now here we were.

"Charley, slow down," Karen said, not for the first time.

Twists and turns. Dips and rises. I roared past a massive open air amphitheater, straddled two lanes as I slowed incrementally out of respect for a Japanese tea garden, revved my engine again as I thundered past a glass-domed art museum that had long since been converted to a municipal office building. All the while, Frank hung tight behind me while Karen closed her eyes and drew one sharp breath after another.

A left turn in front of opposing traffic and two blocks later, Frank and I were neck and neck, rumbling over broken stretches of asphalt. Up ahead, the imposing stone walls of the Academy loomed over the neighborhood, the polished white façade of the Church of Saint Leonard gleaming in the morning sun. If I ran a pointless stop sign and went the wrong way down a one-way street, I could beat Frank hands-down, so I took the turn and blew past a stooped-over old woman in giant sunglasses who was pushing a small grocery cart along the sidewalk. Passing under the stone archway that opened into the Academy's courtyard, I slammed on the brakes and screeched to a halt in the faculty parking lot mere seconds before Frank arrived.

"I win, motherfucker!" I shouted, shaking a finger in his direction as I leapt from my car. "I win!"

Billy's face hung larger than life on either side of the church entrance—a real Chairman Mao look, just like the Kibble King had promised. Nazis marched in loose formation in front of the school as a man in a monkey suit unloaded an inflatable trampoline from the back of a truck. Greg's mother was snapping photographs and cooing at everything she saw, but Billy's parents just stared at me, mouths agape, from the steps of the church as my cell phone went off one last time.

"Jesus," I said.

I took an uneasy step backward and slumped against my car.

I sank to the ground and drew my knees to my chest.

Vaguely aware of the people gathering around me, I rocked back and forth and wished the world would go away.

"Either he's dead or my watch has stopped," Neil said to Karen, emerging from the small crowd and reaching for my wrist as if to take my pulse.

"Neil?" I said, slightly dazed. "Can you do me a favor?"

"Sure thing, pal," Neil said. "Whatever you want."

"Can you destroy my cell phone?"

"Consider it done," Neil said.

"Oh, and there's something I've been meaning to tell you."

"Go for it," Neil said.

"I've never actually seen a Marx Brothers movie."

"Well, yeah," Neil said. "That's pretty obvious."

"You knew?" I asked.

"Of course I knew. I've known since tenth grade."

"You could have told me," I said.

"Nah," Neil said, extending a hand to help me up. "It was more fun to watch you fake it."

ℒ CHAPTER TWENTY ℒ

"There's our guy," Ennis said, smiling broadly and reaching out to shake my hand as I scanned the church for an empty pew.

The man was old, I realized—much older than I usually pictured him. In my mind, he was always my biology professor, a looming presence in a powder-blue lab coat who took no end of pleasure in reminding me that I couldn't skin a cat to save my life. But here, in the flesh, I noticed for the first time how much his face appeared to droop and sag despite his best efforts to maintain a stiff upper lip, how cold and bony his hands felt when he wrapped his fingers around mine, how rigidly he walked, how often he stopped to catch his breath.

"I'll have you know that none of this would have happened without Charley," Ennis said, winking conspiratorially at Karen. "Your husband's a real go-getter."

"Not to mention a maniac behind the wheel," Frank said, clapping Ennis on the shoulder. "Our boy Schwartz could probably drive for NASCAR."

My first instinct was to say something biting in response, but what would it accomplish? We'd been playing this game for so long, making wisecracks and coming up with clever comebacks until we were blue in the face, and where did it get us? I was twice as old as the child I'd been when Frank talked me into making goofy faces for our freshman portrait, but I was still behaving as if no time had passed at all. If I were still fourteen, I'd probably think it sounded like the greatest thing in the world—like hanging on to my youth forever, like always being cool, like never selling out. At twenty-eight, it was nothing short of pathetic.

So I played along with Frank and Ennis—chuckling awkwardly at the joke about my driving, accepting praise for turning Billy's memorial service into a three-ring circus— and when the time came for me to say a few words, I took a breath and shuffled, weak in the knees, up the long, marble aisle that ran the length of the church. My anger over Billy's death still tickled the back of my throat like a nagging cough, but when I took to the rostrum and reached for the microphone, all I could do was remind myself to breathe.

"I took a trip," I said. "To the bridge where Billy killed himself. I don't know what I was looking for, but what I found was sad and lonely, and all I could think about was how angry I was. At the world. At Billy. At myself."

No, I thought as my throat tightened and I choked out the last word. This was wrong. I couldn't—I shouldn't—let anyone see me like this. Breaking down. Losing control. This wasn't me at all. I was the smartass. I was the cynic. I was the misanthrope. I was the guy who never took anything seriously.

But this?

It was real.

Almost too real.

Too real, in any case, to shrug off.

I looked at Billy's parents, perhaps for the first time. His father looked exactly like Billy, or the man Billy would have become if he'd ever gotten the chance to grow old— skinny and graying, a humble smile in a three-button suit. His mother was a tiny woman who kept her head bowed low and held a leather-bound photo album in her arms as if she were holding a baby.

"I could have been a better friend," I said. "We all could have been better friends. Not just to Billy, but to each other, too. We were practically babies when we came to Saint Leonard's. Thirteen, fourteen years old. Pretending to be men. Pretending we knew what we were doing when all we were was scared."

I cleared my throat, sure I'd start to fall apart at any second.

"So we played these games," I said. "Stupid games. Cruel games. Games that boys play when all they want to do is let the world know how tough they are, how smart, how funny, how good with women."

I bit the inside of my mouth and tried to hold on.

"But not Billy," I said. "He was quiet and shy and never went in for that kind of stuff. Putting on airs, I mean. Acting like he knew it all, like a tough guy, like he could handle anything."

I looked at Karen. I looked at Neil. I wanted to say I was sorry for all I'd ever put them through, sorry for playing games all the time, sorry for turning everything into a joke, and sorry, most of all, for acting so often like I was still fourteen years old.

"We had a cat one year," I said. "In biology class. After the worm and the frog and the fetal pig, they gave us a cat, and Billy named it Fascia. To me it was just another prop, something to cut open and poke around in, but to Billy it was almost holy. Like—I don't know—like the cat had given its life to teach him something. Like he owed some kind of respect to the cat. Like the least he could do was treat the cat with kindness, even in death."

Time was slipping away from me.

Time was *always* slipping away.

"I wish I could tell you more," I said. "I wish I could stand here and say this was Billy, and this is why he was special and this is why the world is worse without him, but I can't. All I can ask is that you remember him kindly. Remember our friend and the example he set. Remember his kindness. Remember his love. Remember the delicate light we all took for granted, and open your hearts to the wonder of the world. Always be generous. Always be kind. And know that although he's no longer with us, Billy Chin will always be near—watching with interest, smiling down on us, lighting our way. Shining."

When I returned to my pew, Neil laid a hand on my shoulder, and Karen squeezed my fingers. It wasn't until then that I started to cry. Not because I was sad, but not because I was happy either. Because I was both. Because when Neil touched my shoulder and Karen squeezed my fingers, I knew they loved me and that I loved them, just like Billy had loved his parents and they had loved him more than anything in the world. I wanted that moment to last forever, that love, that connection, that feeling beyond words, but I knew there was no way it could because there was time, because there was life, because there was death as well. Because there were always intrusions, deviations, surprises, and interruptions, and even though I loved Karen and Neil and wanted more than anything to hold them close and never let go, I knew it wasn't an option because what I wanted wasn't living, and it wasn't even dying. Because living and dying walk hand in hand, and the alternative to both is neither—cold as a stone, unchanging and lifeless.

AFTER THE service, we all went outside where the red and blue lights of a police cruiser were sweeping the perimeter of the Academy's courtyard as a cop conferred with a Nazi prison guard and the woman with the grocery cart took down the number on my license plate.

"You can leave in a taxi," Neil said as the ersatz Nazi pointed me out to the police officer. "But if you can't get a taxi, you can leave in a huff. And if that's too soon, you can leave in a minute and a huff."

Animal Crackers, I wondered?

"Don't worry," Dwayne Coleman said on his way out of the church. "I'll handle this."

Flashing his badge, Dwayne intercepted the officer. Was the old woman's complaint legitimate, he asked? Certainly. Were there any other witnesses? No. Had I, in fact, driven the wrong way down a one-way street? Absolutely. Did I have a good reason for doing so? Not at all. Would arresting me take a dangerous driver off the road? Without a doubt. Was it worth the paperwork on a Saturday morning? Highly unlikely.

"Have fun in the big house," Neil murmured, but the officer was already leaving the scene.

When Phil Ennis was sure no one was being arrested, he invited us all into the school where, thanks to my efforts, a hundred-odd strangers, mostly children, were already milling about the lobby and the adjoining gymnasium—climbing on artificial rocks, throwing darts at balloons, tossing tiny plastic rings over the necks of glass coke bottles, and punching Mr. Monkeybounce in the nuts because he couldn't get his trampoline to inflate properly. Standing on a small riser in the lobby, Ennis thanked everyone for coming and launched into his usual speech about what a wonderful place the Academy was and what a great job the school did when it came to molding young men into the leaders of the future. Young men like Billy Chin, he added, who would have been so glad to see all his friends coming together to celebrate his life at the school he loved so much.

I looked at Neil, and he shrugged as if to say this was who Ennis was and that we couldn't expect any more or any less from him. I shrugged back, and a skinny kid from the neighborhood pressed an envelope into my hand. *Yes!* it read. *I would like to make a contribution of __$100 __$250 __$500 __$1,000 __ (or more!) to honor the memory of Billy Chin and help Saint Leonard's Academy continue in its tradition of excellence.*

I shook my head and turned to show the envelope to Karen, but she was nowhere to be found. When I asked Neil if he'd seen her, he said that if my wife had received the same invitation that Greg's mother had sent to Madeline, she was probably looking for a safe place to hide. As if to confirm Neil's suspicion, Greg's mother spotted us and made a beeline through the crowd. Where were our wives, she demanded? Were they already inside the theater waiting for the play to start? Pushing children out of her way, she waded up to us and snapped a picture. For posterity, she said. So Greg could remember all the little people when he made it to the big time. One of these days, his picture would be in all the papers, she said. We'd turn on the evening news, and Greg's name would be on everyone's lips.

"That's funny," Neil said. "Sean Sullivan keeps saying the same thing."

"Speaking of which, why isn't he here?"

At the far end of the gym, Dwayne Coleman was attempting to hold a crowd of children at bay while Mr. Monkeybounce writhed on the floor, howling with pain.

"I think he is," Neil said.

Curled up in a ball and clad in a monkey suit, Sean held two furry hands over his testicles as Dwayne shooed little kids away from him. Having suffered a similar brand of humiliation back when I was a dollar sign, I was particularly attuned to Sean's pain, so I joined in the fray and helped Dwayne drive the hopped-up hordes of angry young children away from my fallen comrade and his malfunctioning trampoline.

"Shoot me," Sean moaned as Neil helped him to his feet. "I mean it, Dwayne. Put me out of my misery. I'm dying."

"Not today, pal," Neil said as the lights in the gym flashed like lightning.

"Jesus," Sean moaned. "It's the end of the world."

"Not quite," Neil said, pulling the mask from Sean's face to give him some air. "But it may be the end of legitimate theater as we know it."

"Dare we?" Dwayne said as the crowd started swirling through the theater doors like water down a drain.

"I don't think so," I said. "I've had enough drama for a while."

THE LAST thing I expected to hear was laughter, but there it was. First, a soft, rolling lilt that made me think of children at play. This was Karen's laugh, but there was another one, too—a woman whose voice sounded vaguely familiar. Maybe Madeline. Maybe someone else. Then a third and a fourth, a snort and a chuckle. A man's laugh, like a crow, and a whinny, like a horse. This was music. This was song. Five-part harmony in a dozen different keys, and my first instinct was to silence it.

This was no time for laughter, I wanted to say, burning with self-righteous indignation. This was no time for joy. My friend was dead, and I'd turned his memorial service into a massive roadside spectacle. What business, I was ready to demand as I worked my way through the crowd with my best friend, a cop, and a gorilla in tow, did anyone have laughing under such circumstances?

That Karen's voice was among the guilty only added to my rage. She was my wife, for God's sake. I thought I knew her. If anyone would have the common decency to maintain a certain level of decorum and behave with at least a modicum of respect, it would be her. I wouldn't single her out, of course, but in my mind I was already pulling Karen aside and asking how she thought Billy's parents would feel if they could hear her laughing at their son's memorial service. Zeroing in on the source of the jocularity, however, I realized the point was moot. Billy's parents were right there with her, along with Madeline Pogue and Maya Dearborn. They were seated around a small, gray table in the school cafeteria, each with a hand on Mrs. Chin's photo album. On the page in front of them, her son was five years old and wore a wide smile despite the fact that he was missing two front teeth.

"He had a name for every squirrel in the neighborhood," Billy's mother was saying. "He used to call them his outside pets."

They all laughed again—Karen and Madeline, Maya, Billy's parents. Frank Dearborn was lurking in the background, watching his wife for cues. He smiled when she smiled, laughed when she laughed, and I wondered if she made him more human.

"Charley," Karen said when she saw me. "Come look at these pictures of Billy."

Billy's mother looked up, and so did his father. They were both smiling, their eyes wet with tears.

"I've been meaning to talk to you," I said. "I should have called. I should have asked if this was what you wanted."

"Sit with us," Billy's mother said. "Please."

The table was crowded, but everyone squeezed together to make room for me, and Frank Dearborn grabbed a chair from an adjoining table.

"Come on, Schwartz. Have a seat," he said.

Neil was standing next to me. The other guys weren't too far behind. This one was my call—take the seat or hold on to my grief. As if one necessarily precluded the other. But playing the martyr had come so easily. I could rant and rave and roar at the world for screwing Billy at every turn. I could hate myself for failing Billy in his time of need. I could even stand in front of everyone and adopt the wise demeanor of someone who had experienced loss and was only now learning to deal with it, but none of that was about Billy. It was all about me. If I really wanted to honor his memory, if I really wanted to move on, if I really believed in mercy and compassion and all the stuff I talked about when I had the world's attention, I'd sit down with Billy's parents and my wife and my best friend and my sworn enemy, and I'd look at pictures of Billy and smile and laugh and cry and remember what a wonderful human being he really was.

"I didn't know it would turn out like this," I said. "I didn't know everything would get so out of hand."

"He was sick," Billy's father said. "There was nothing you could have done."

I took the seat that Frank offered and sat down next to Karen. She put a hand on my knee, and I wrapped my fingers around hers as Billy's mother turned the pages of her photo album and we watched her little boy grow into the young man we all wished we'd known a little better.